THOR™

AN ORIGIN STORY

Based on the Marvel comic book series **Thor**
Adapted by Rich Thomas Jr.
Illustrated by Val Semeiks *and* Hi-Fi Design

New York • Los Angeles

marvelkids.com

© 2013 MARVEL

Case Illustrated by Pat Olliffe and Brian Miller
Designed by Jason Wojtowicz

Printed in the United States of America
Second Edition
1 3 5 7 9 10 6 8 4 2
G942-9090-6-13227
ISBN 978-1-4231-7215-4

SUSTAINABLE FORESTRY INITIATIVE

Certified Sourcing
www.sfiprogram.org
SFI-00993
For Text Only

What would it be like to live among **gods**?
To be something **more** than human?

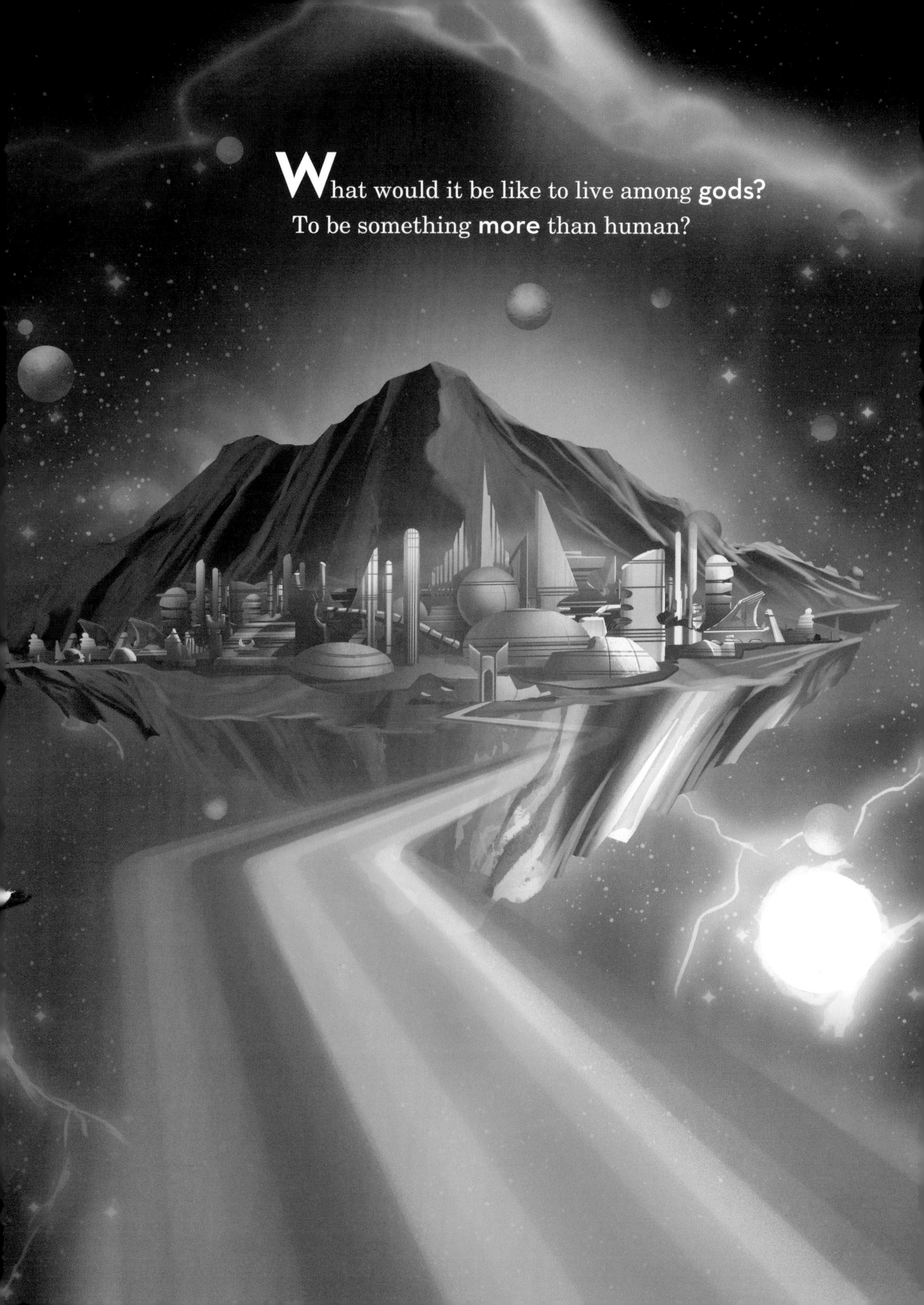

To hold **great power** in your hand

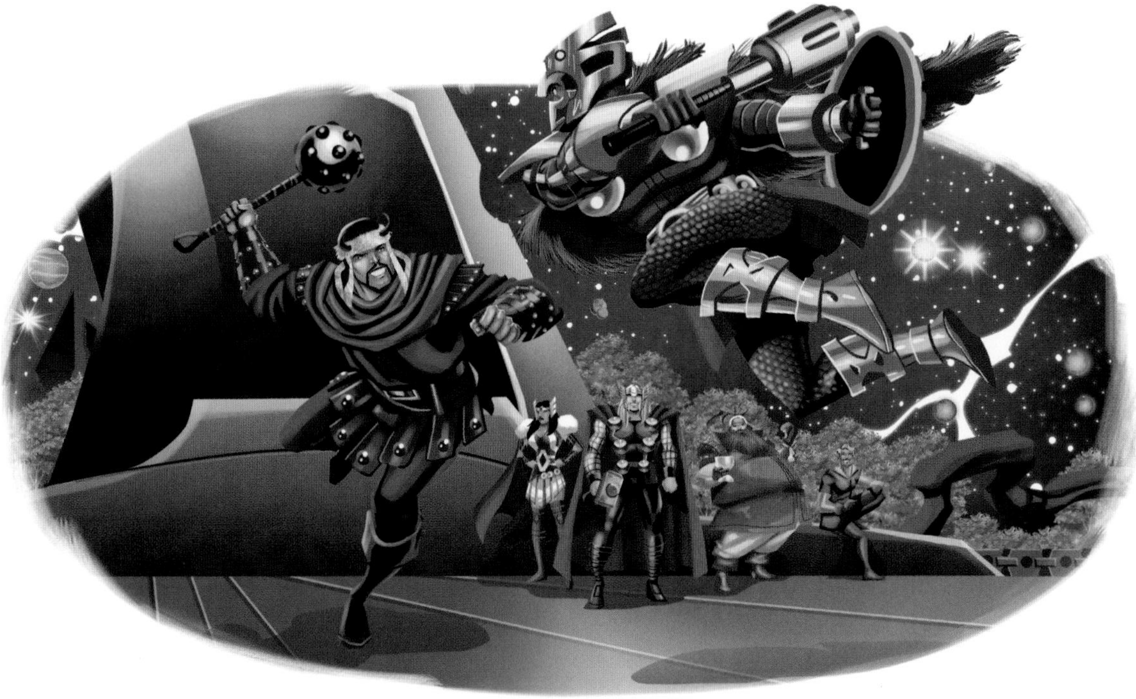

and know how to **use** it?

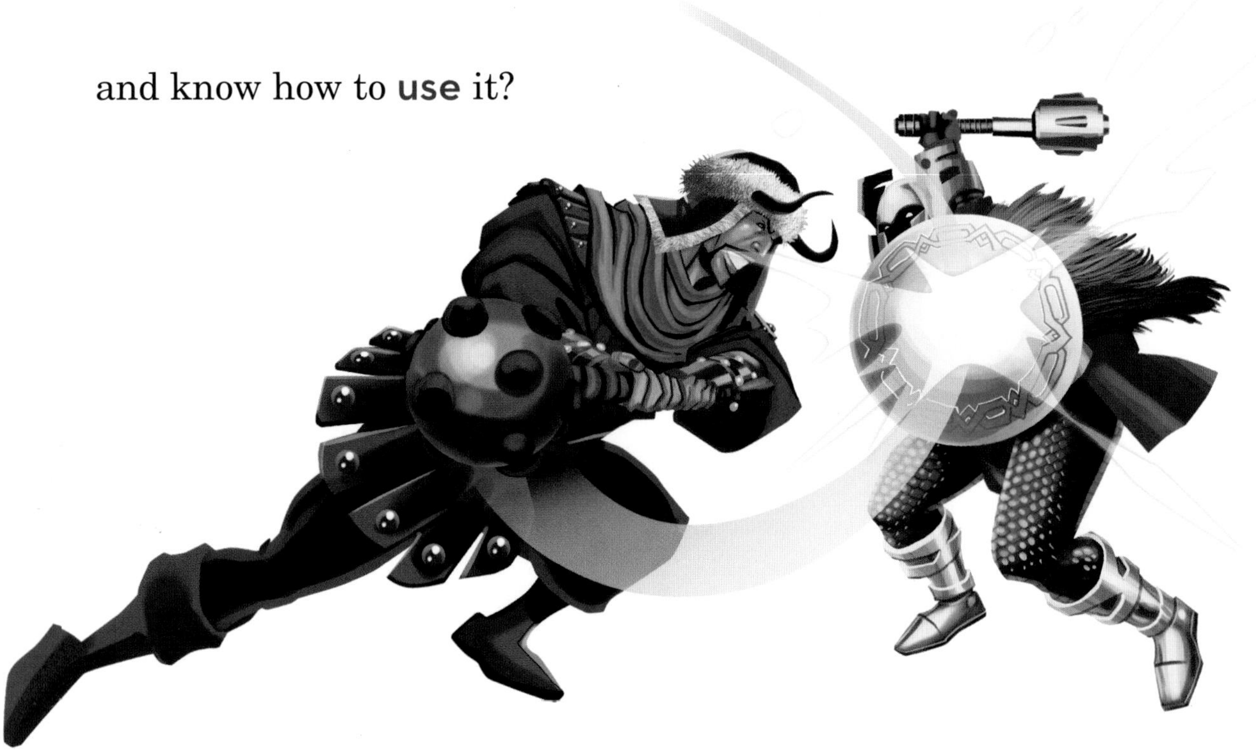

To be **FEARED**?

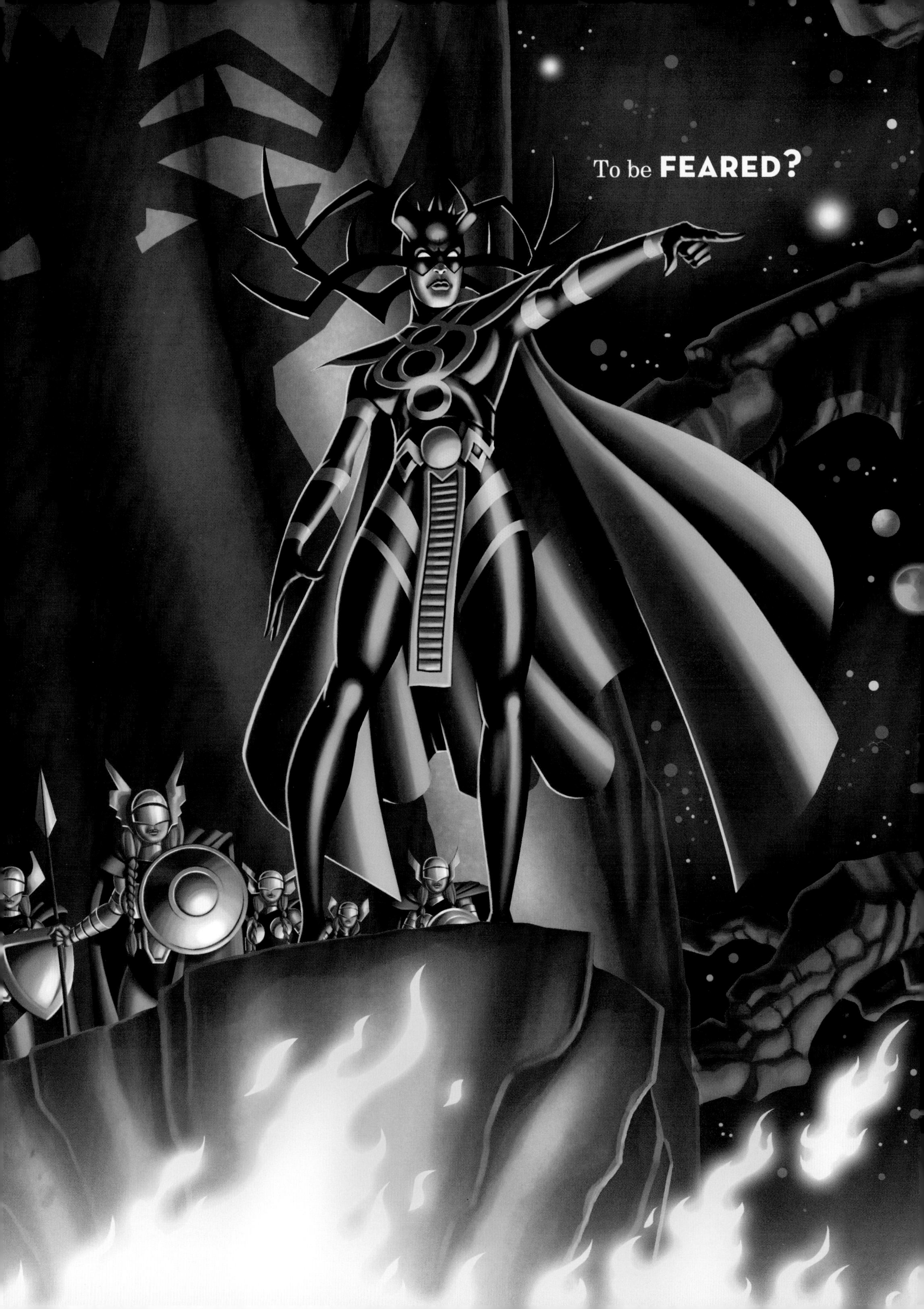

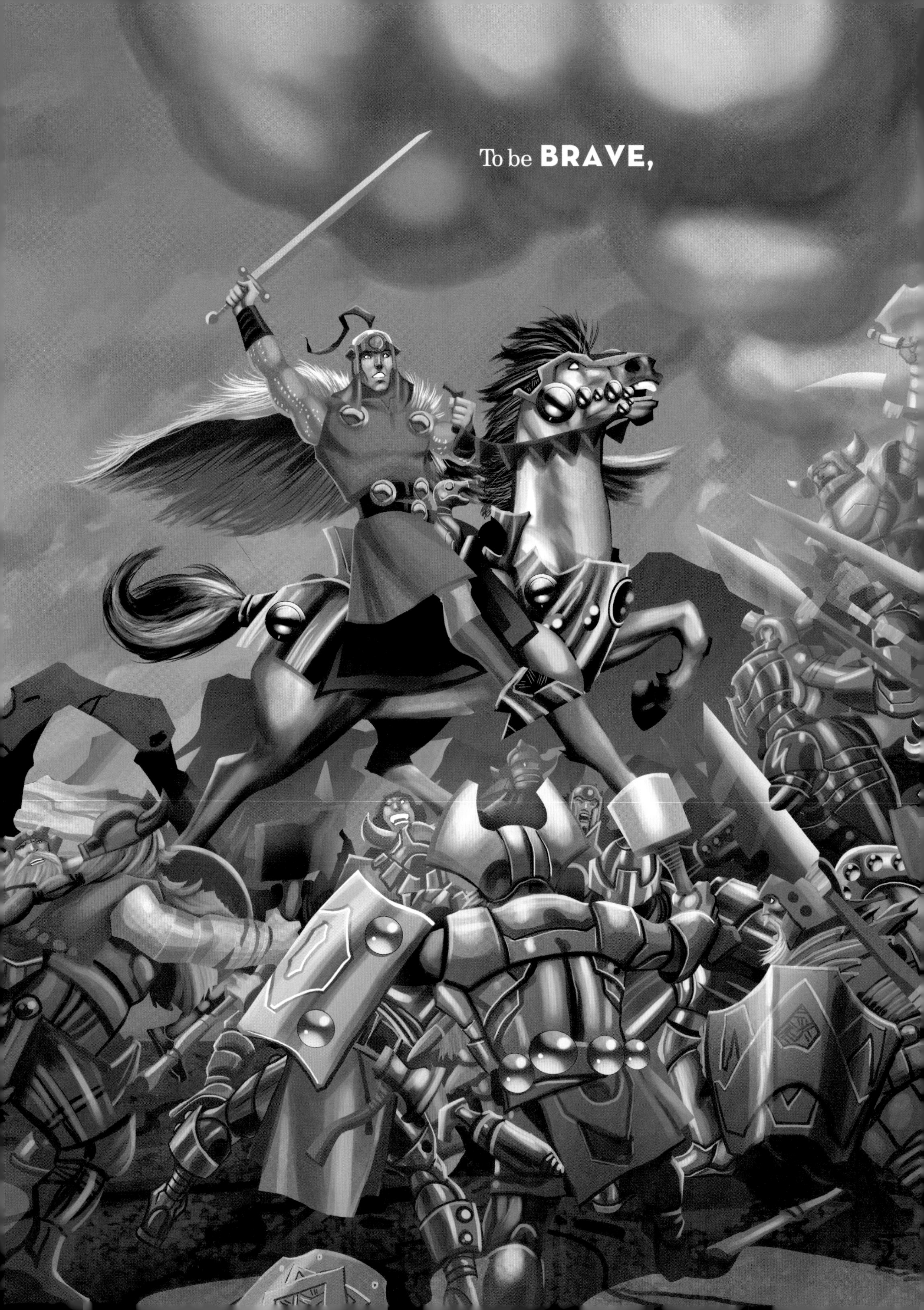

To be **BRAVE,**

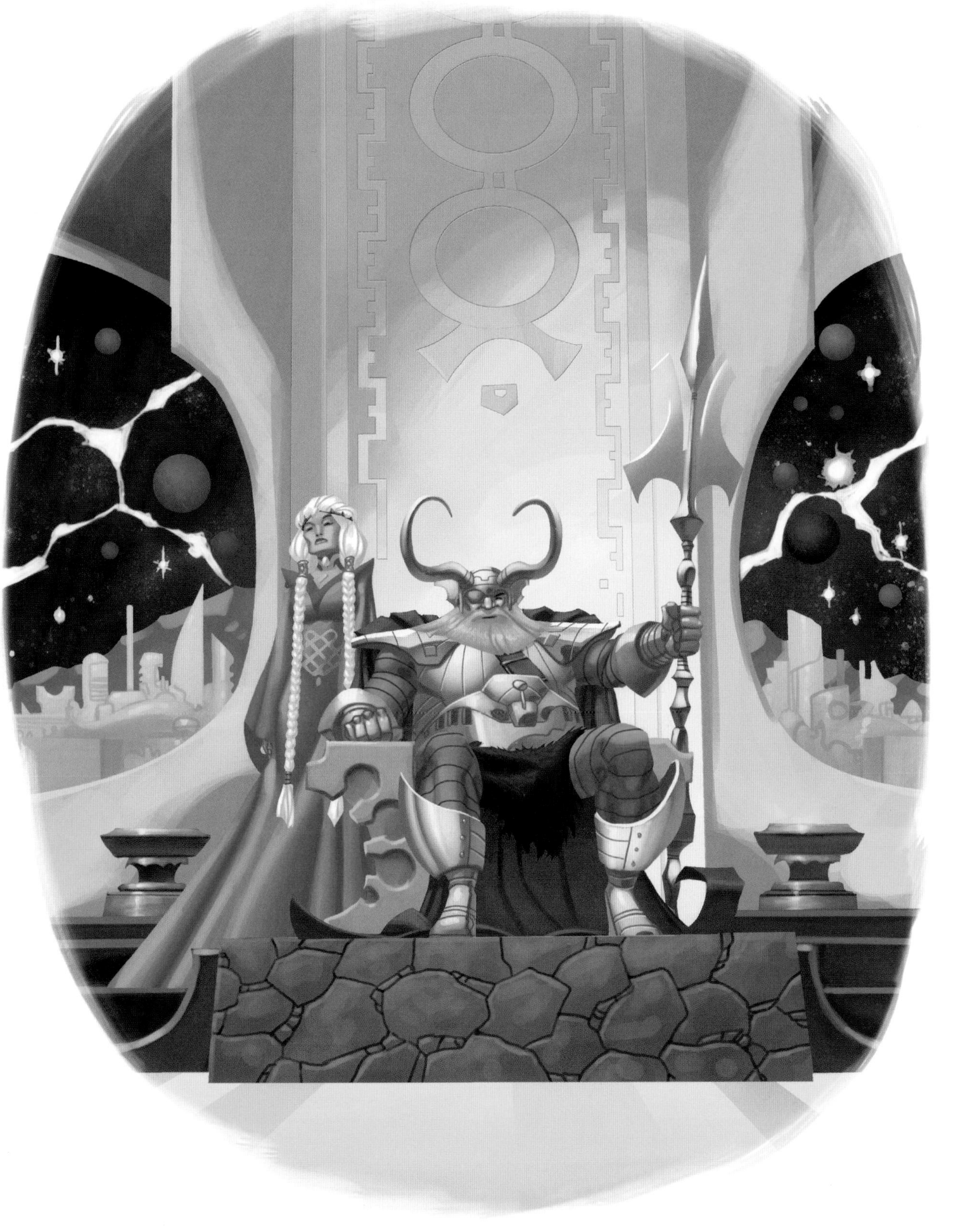

to be **HONORED—**

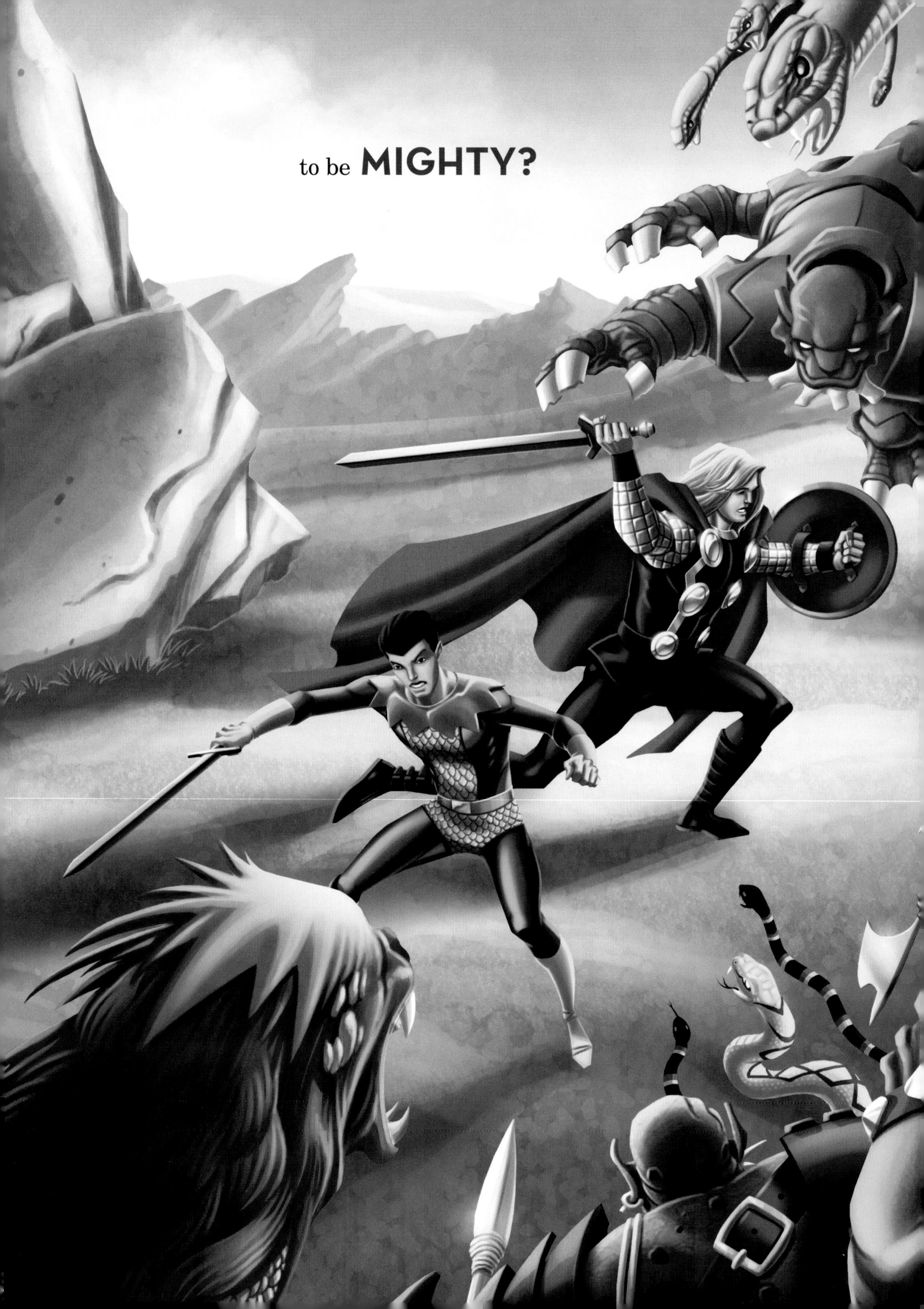
to be MIGHTY?

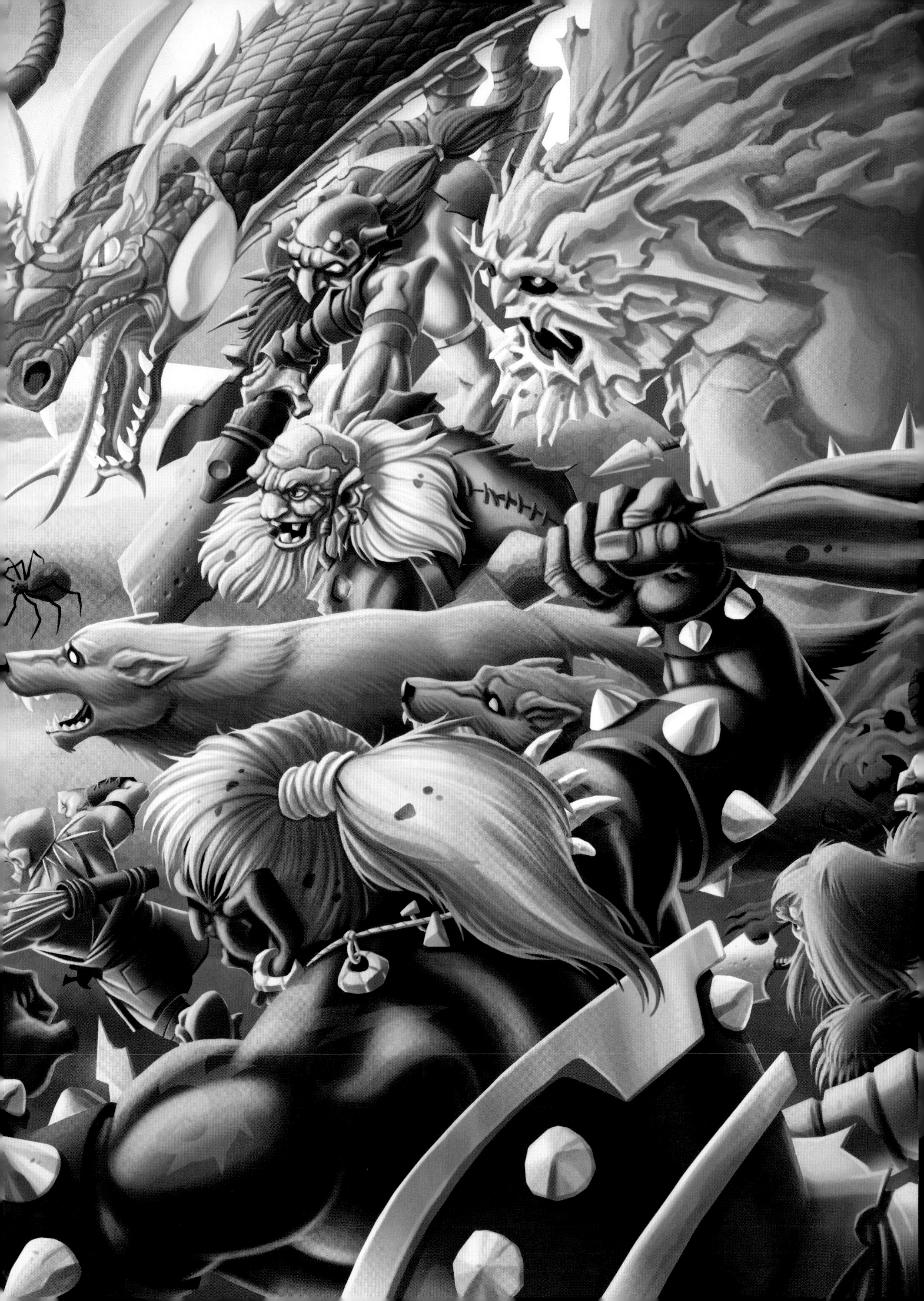

Some are **born** with these qualities.

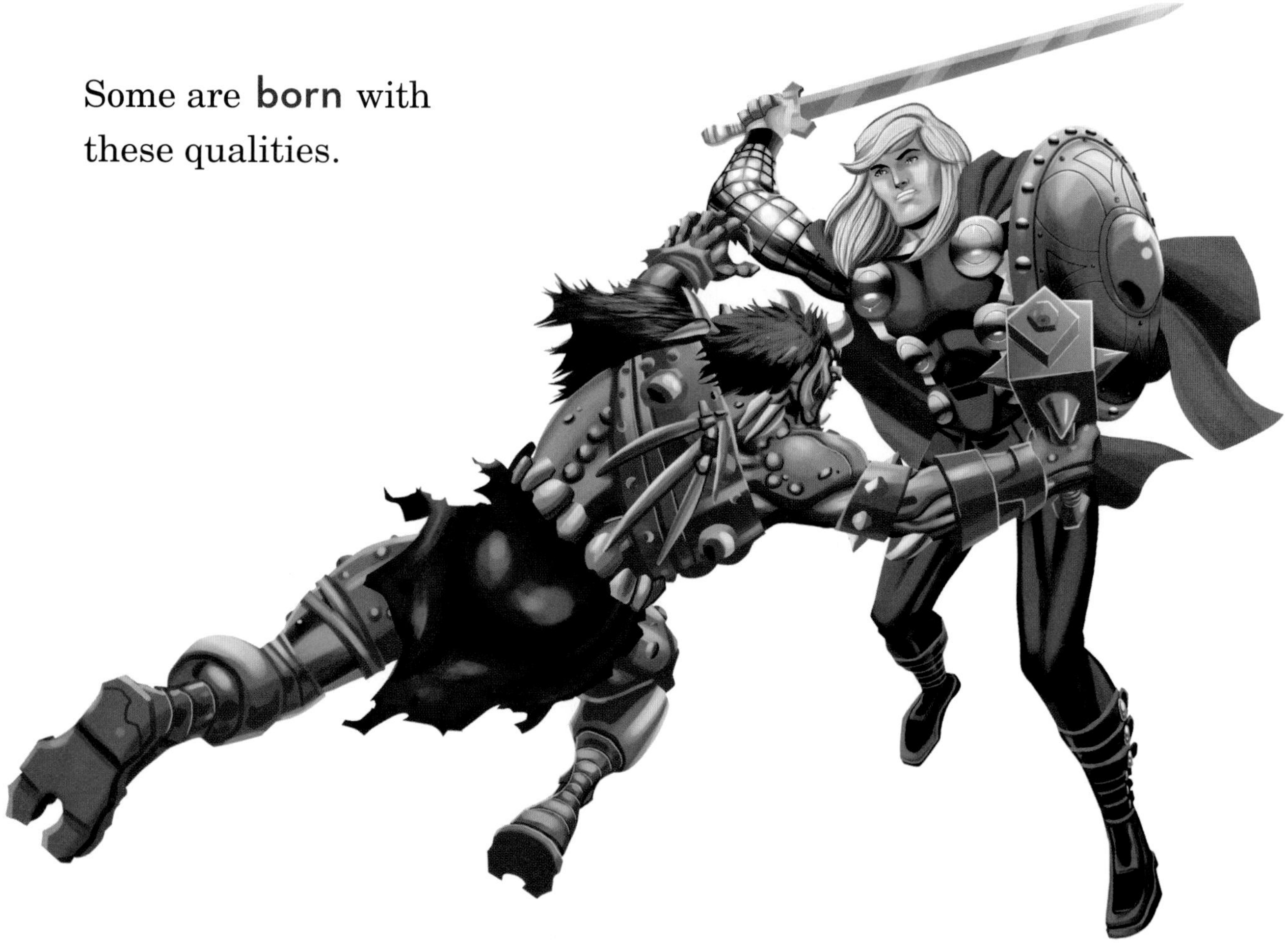

And some spend their lives **working** to attain them.

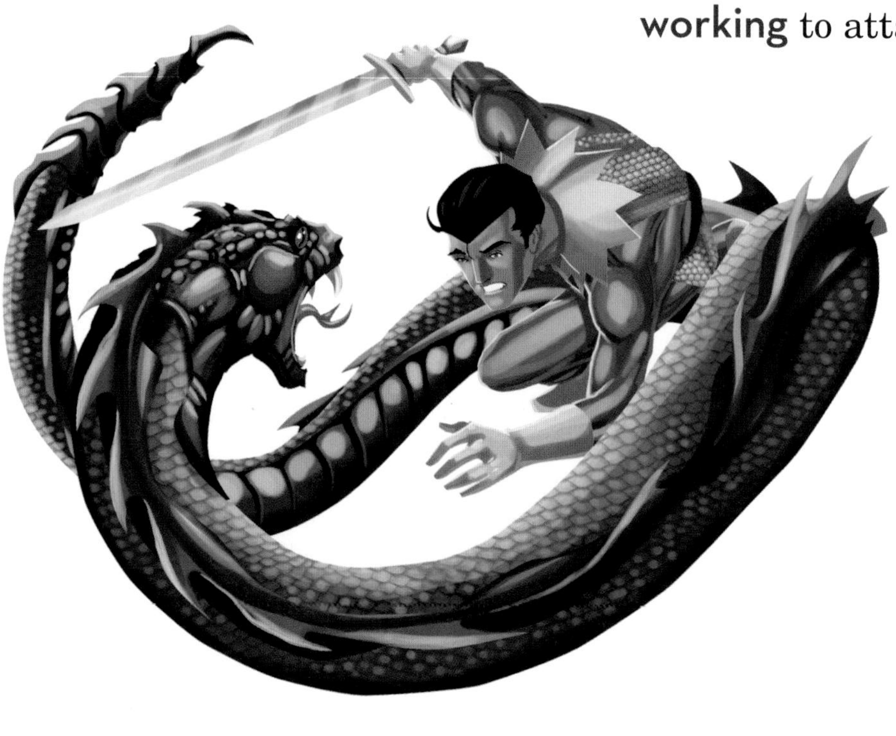

This is a story about someone who was born into royalty **but needed to earn his honor.**

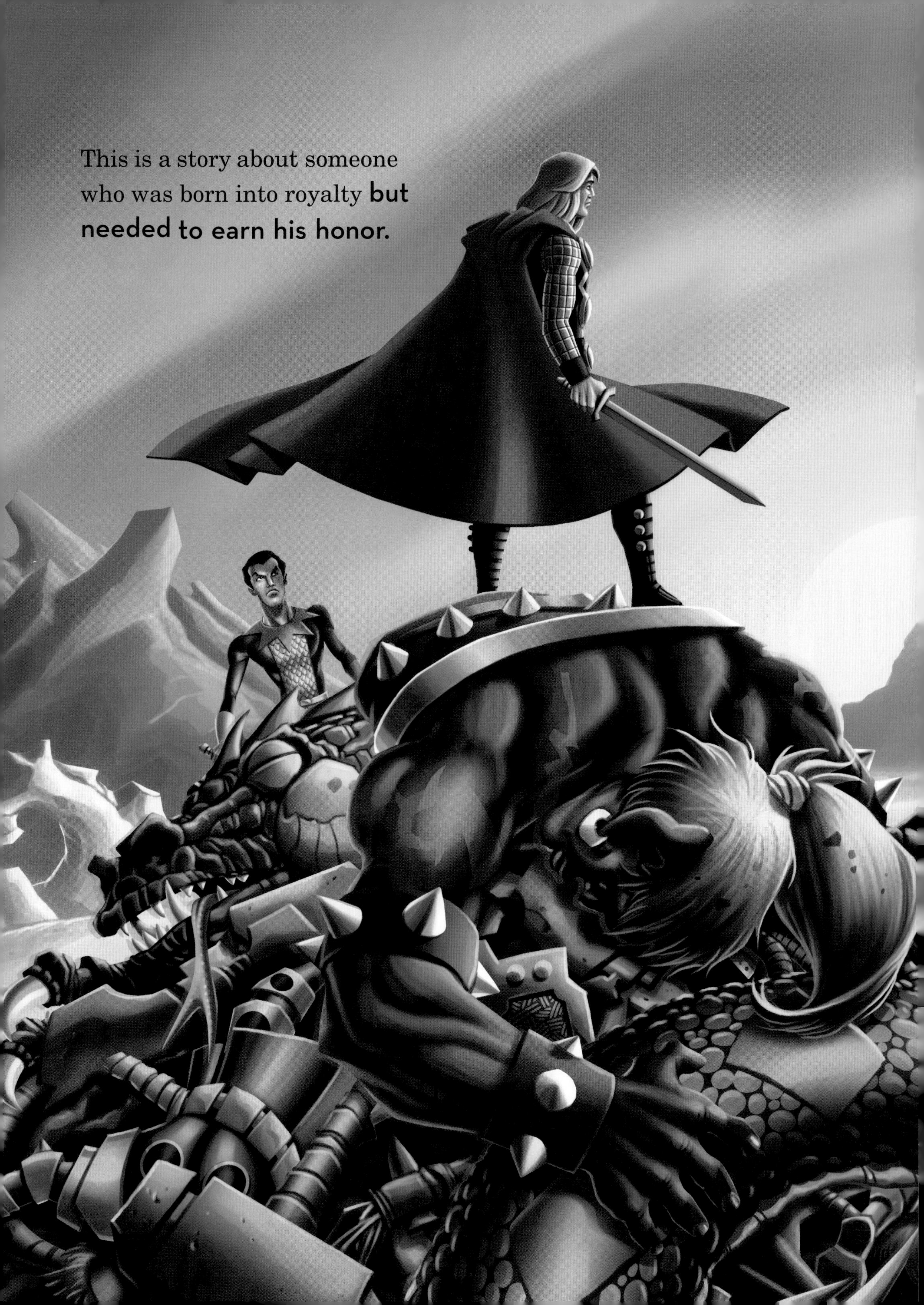

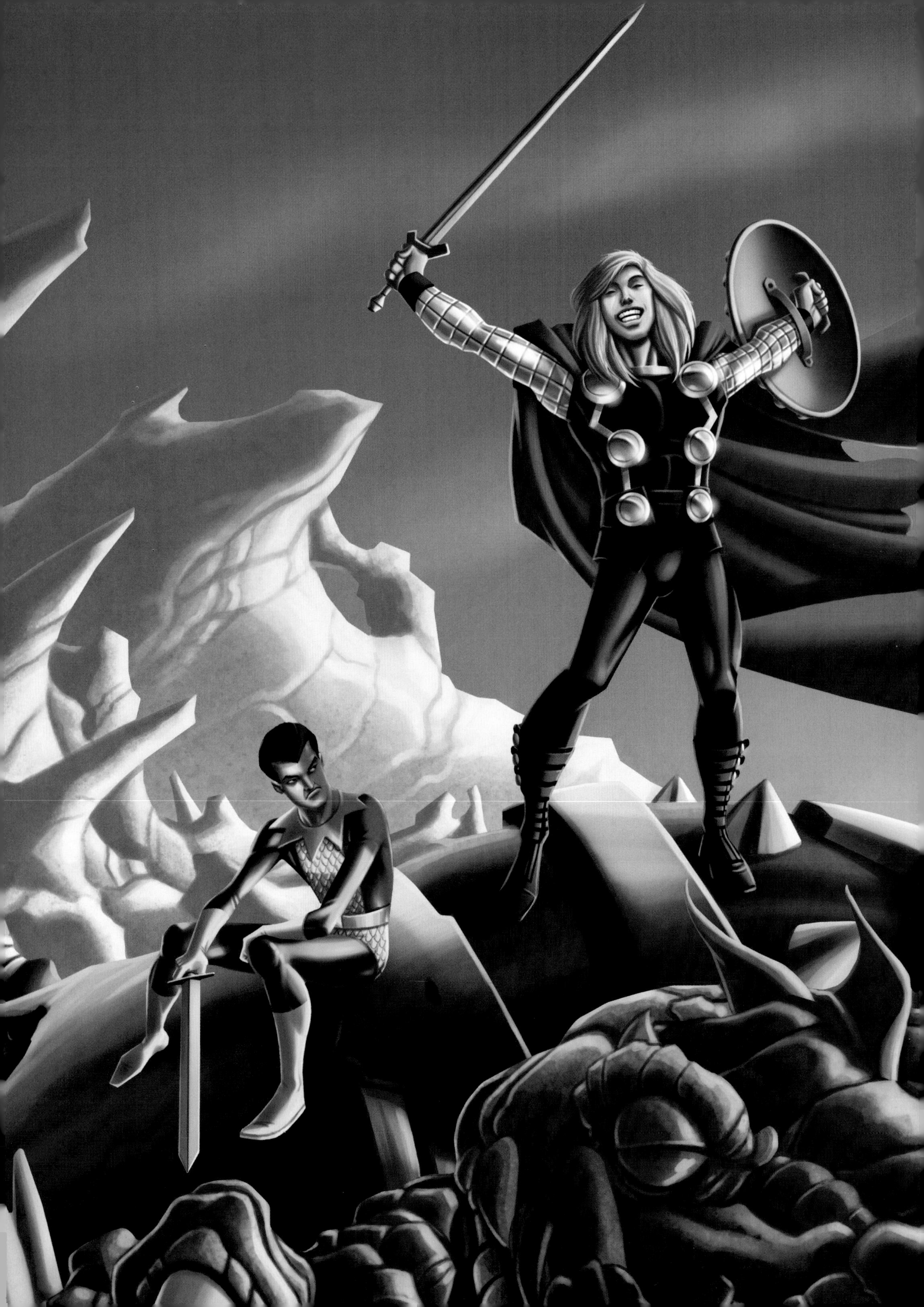

This is a story about a hero named **THOR.**

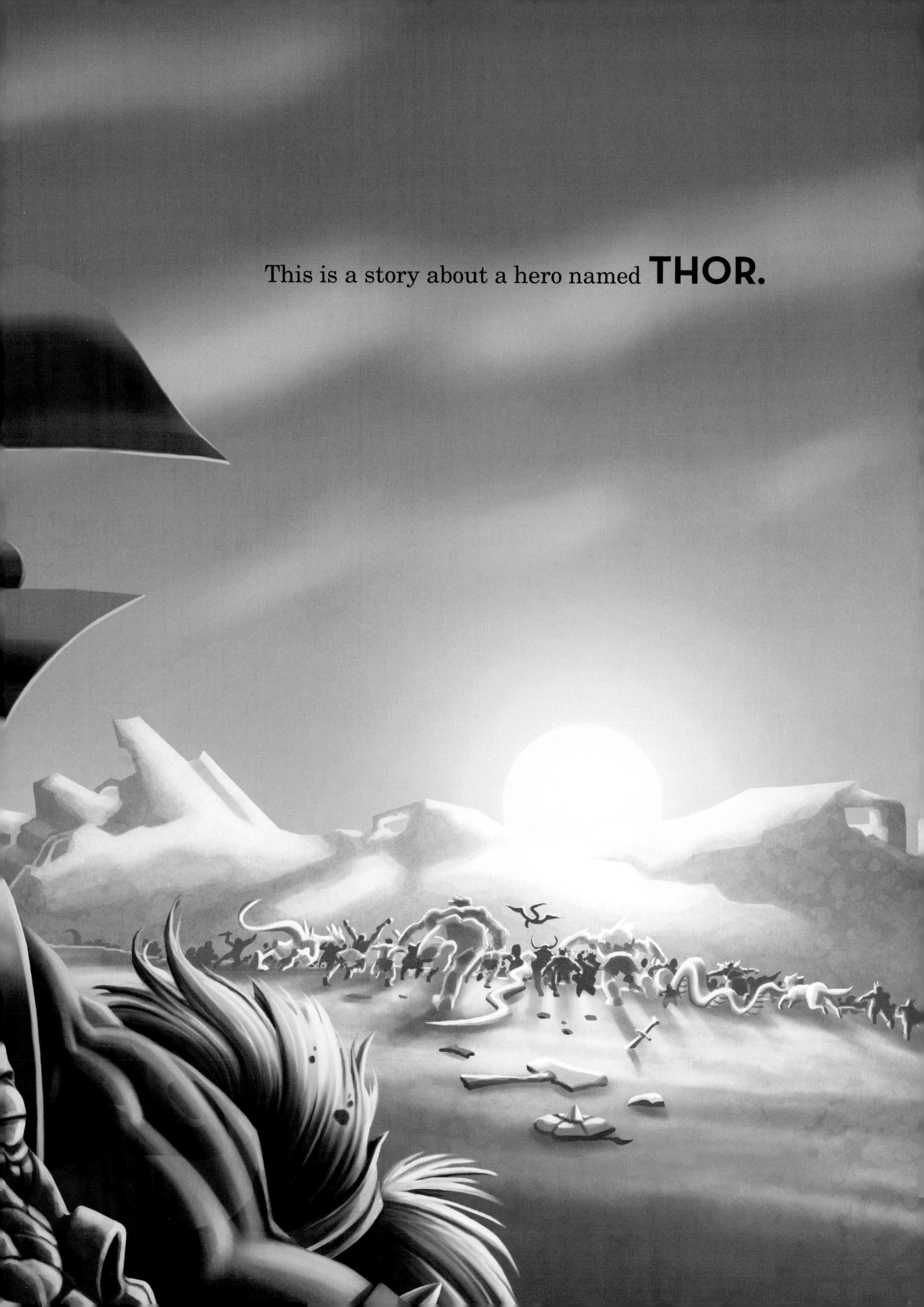

Thor's realm was called **Asgard,** meaning "home of the gods."

It sat like an island whose shores were swept by the sea of space.

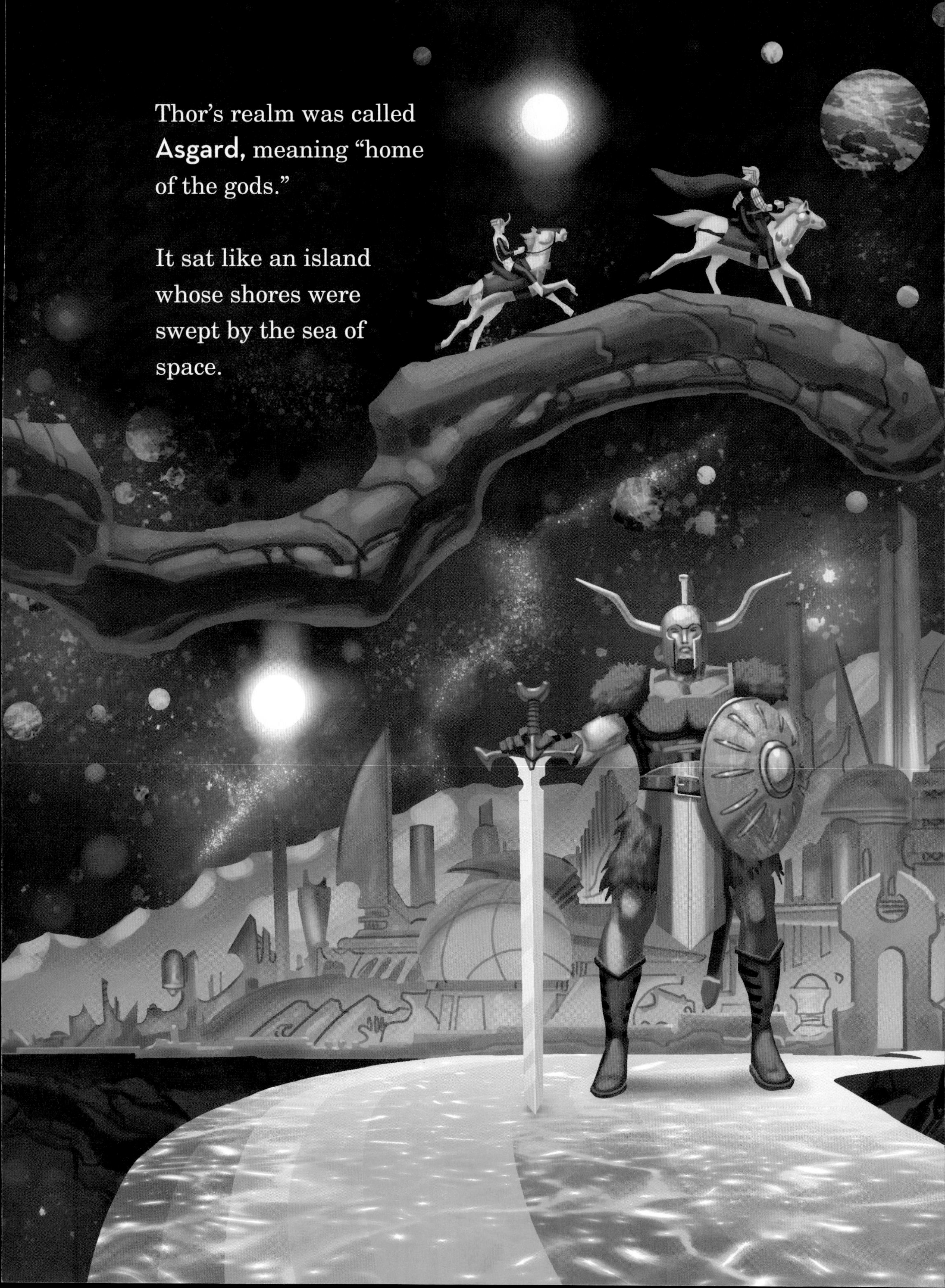

The people who lived on Asgard were called **Asgardians,** and the Asgardians called our world **Midgard.** The only way to reach our world from theirs was by the rainbow bridge, Bifrost. And Bifrost was guarded by the sentry called **Heimdall.**

But even though Asgard was well-protected from the outside, threats from inside its gates were endless. And **Thor** was one of the land's **great protectors.**

Thor was also a prince. He lived with his brother Loki in the castle of their father, Odin.

Thor did not have many friends, but the few he did have were loyal: the brave warrior **Balder,** the beautiful and strong **Lady Sif,** and a band of soldiers called the Warriors Three— **Fandral, Hogun,** and **Volstagg.**

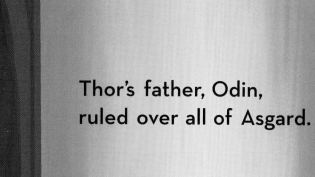

Thor's father, Odin, ruled over all of Asgard.

He and his wife, Frigga, wanted nothing more than for their sons to grow up to be worthy rulers.

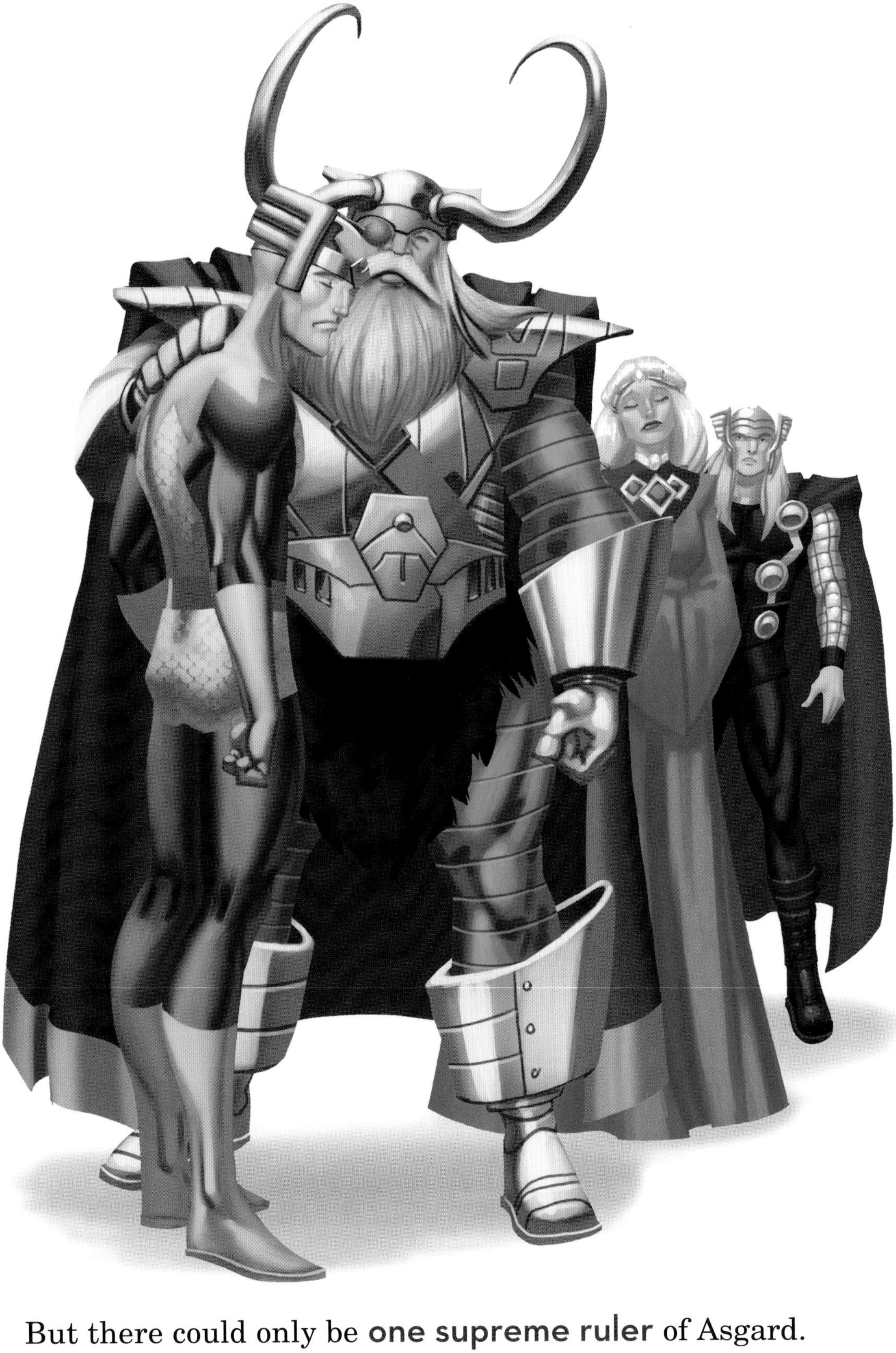

But there could only be **one supreme ruler** of Asgard. Only one who could be like Odin. And even though Loki was thoughtful, clever, and quick . . .

Thor was Odin's **favored son.**

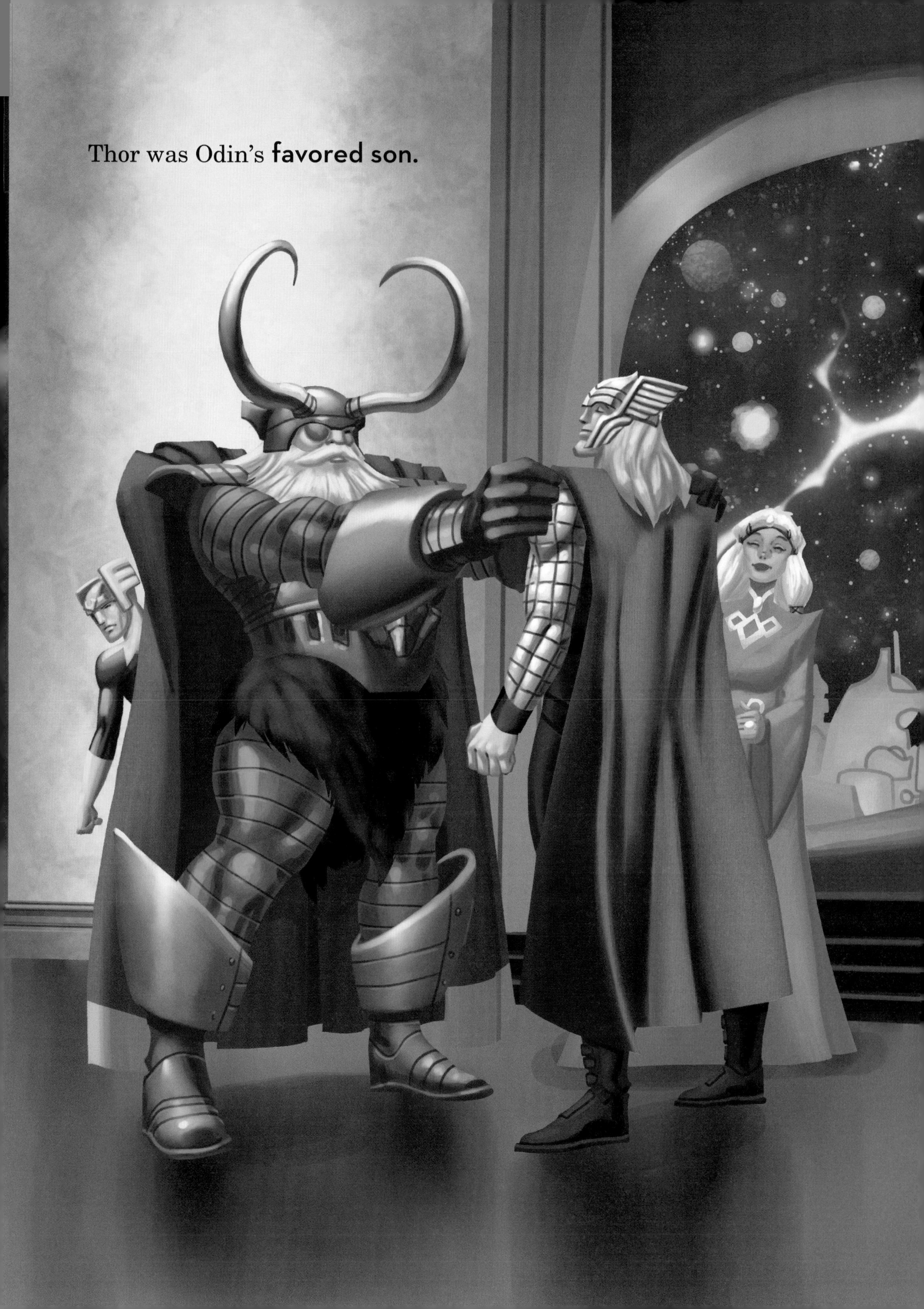

To show his favor, Odin had a special hammer forged from a mystical metal called *Uru*, which came from the heart of a dying star. The hammer was named **Mjolnir,** and it held great power.

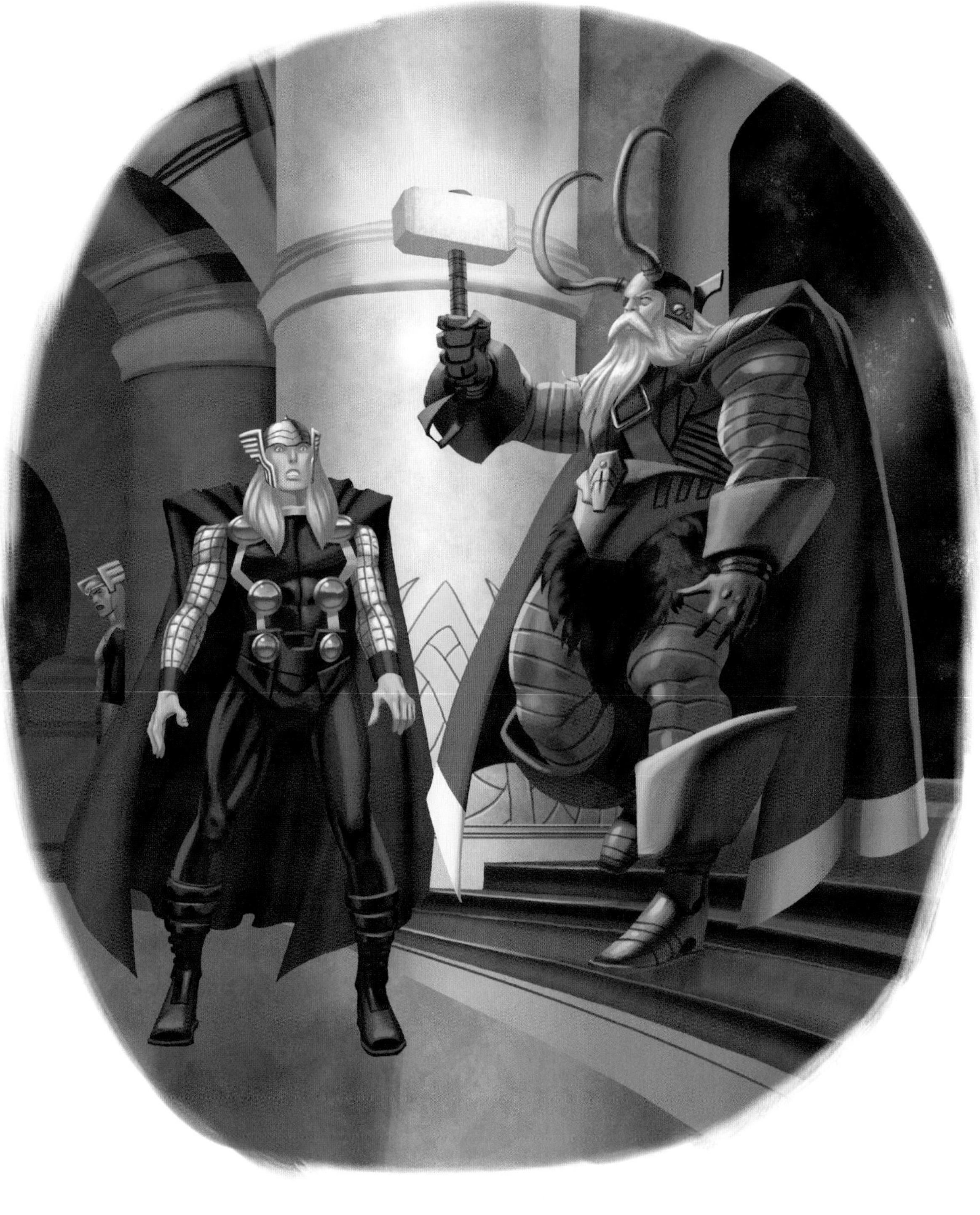

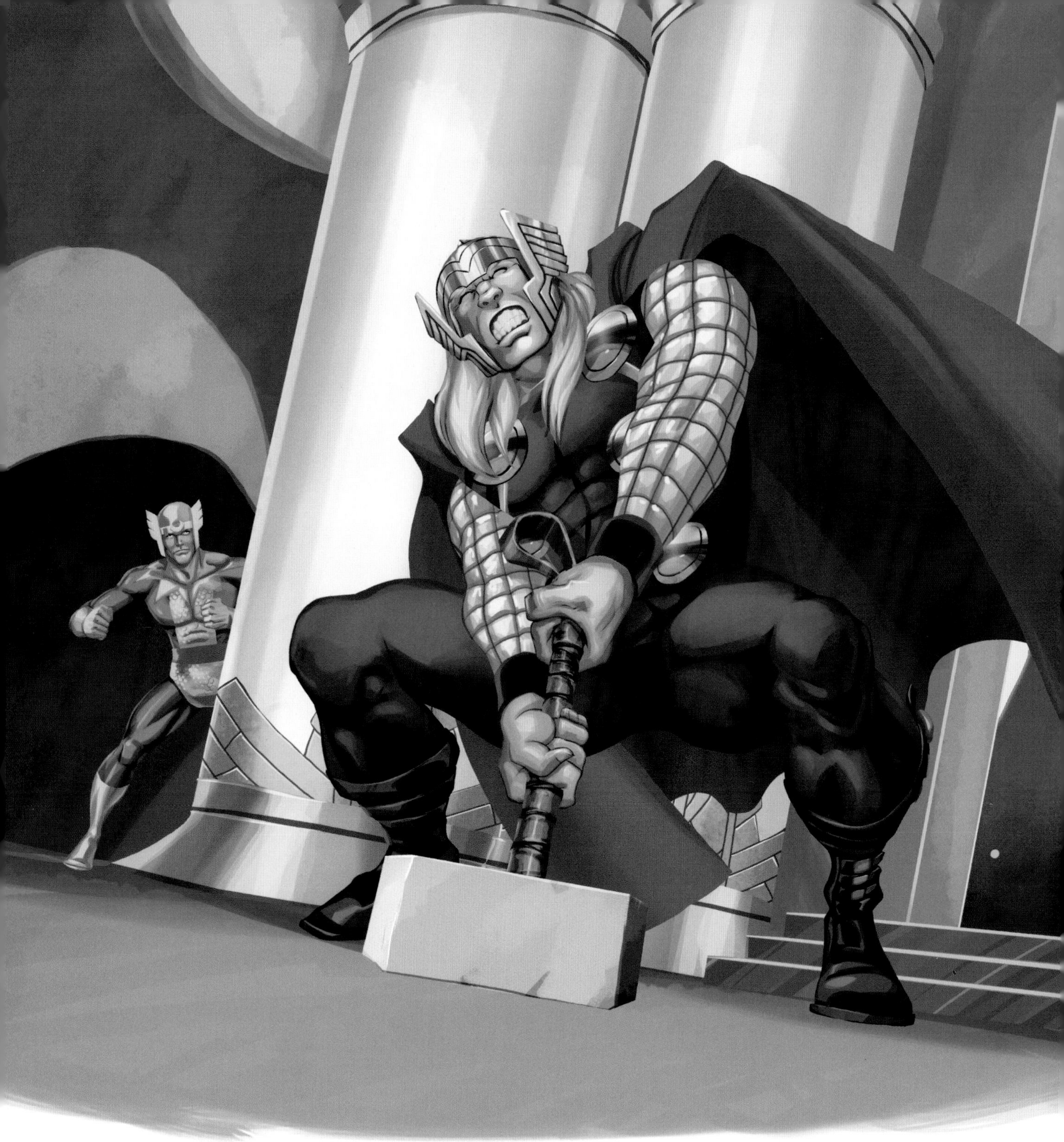

But no one would be able to lift the hammer
unless he or she was worthy.

The hammer seemed **immovable** to Thor.

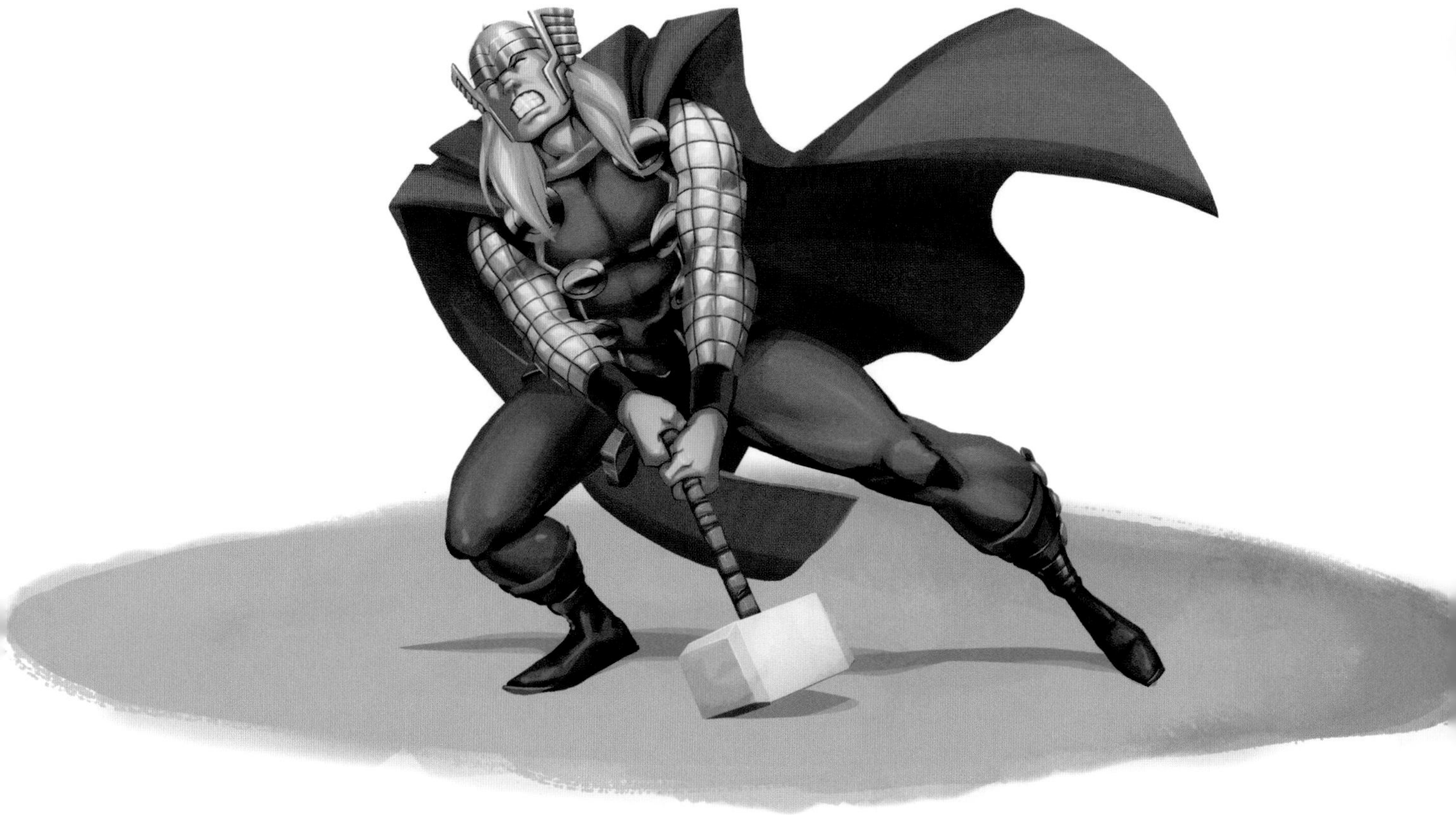

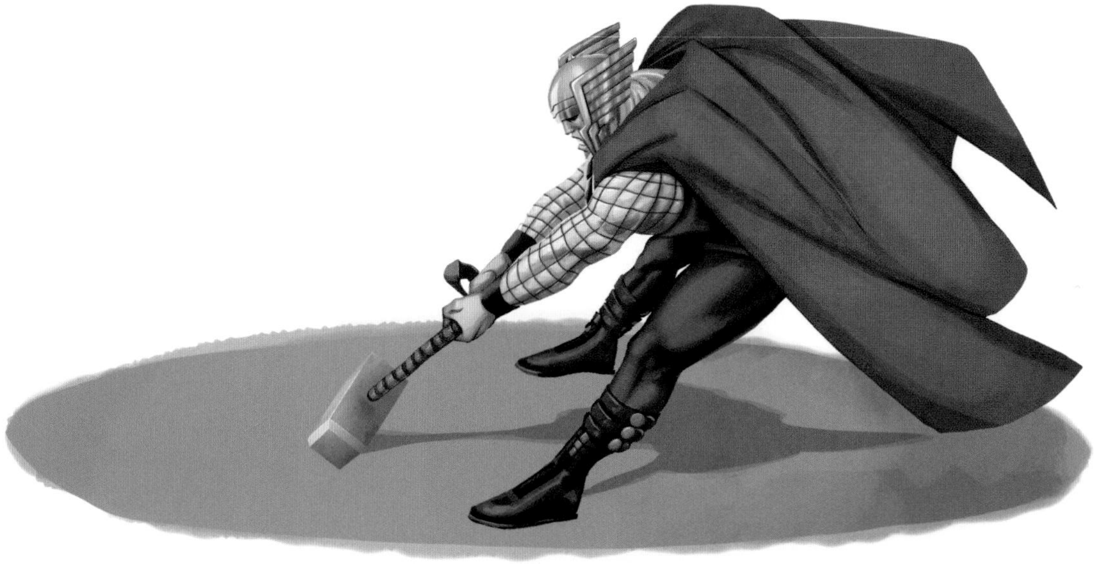

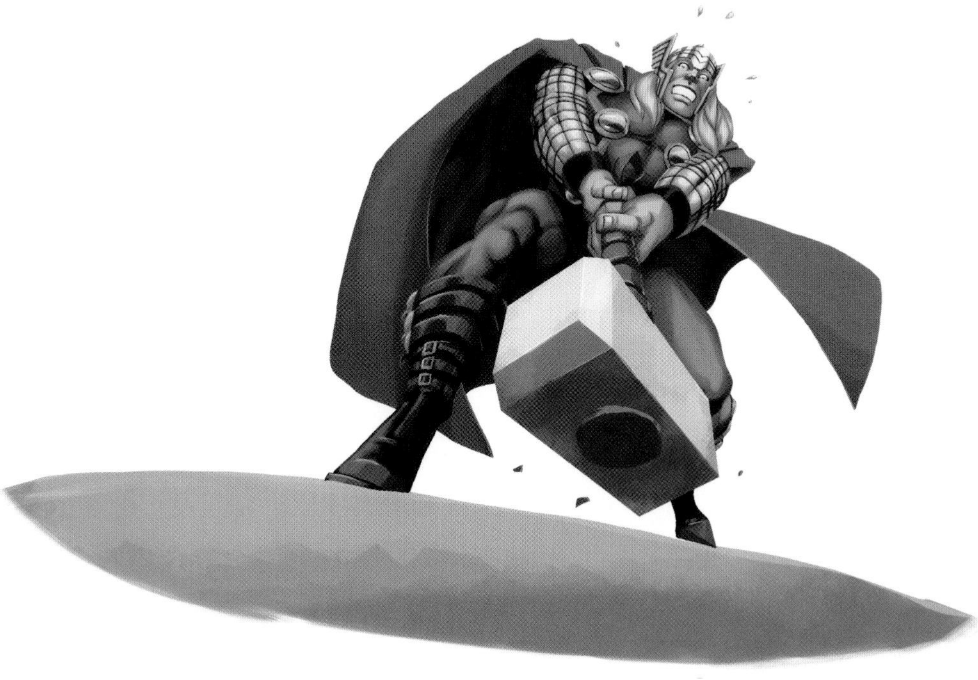

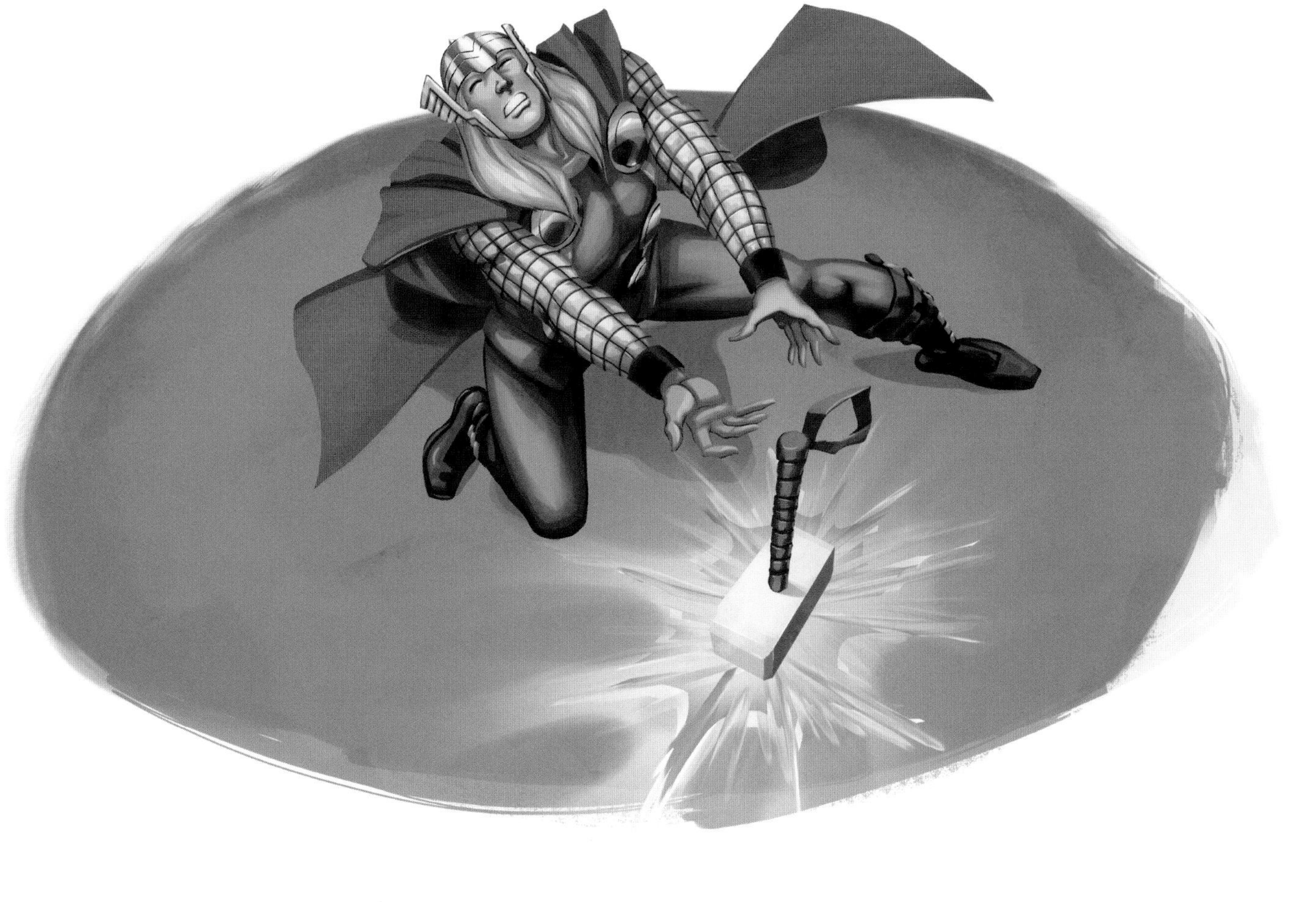

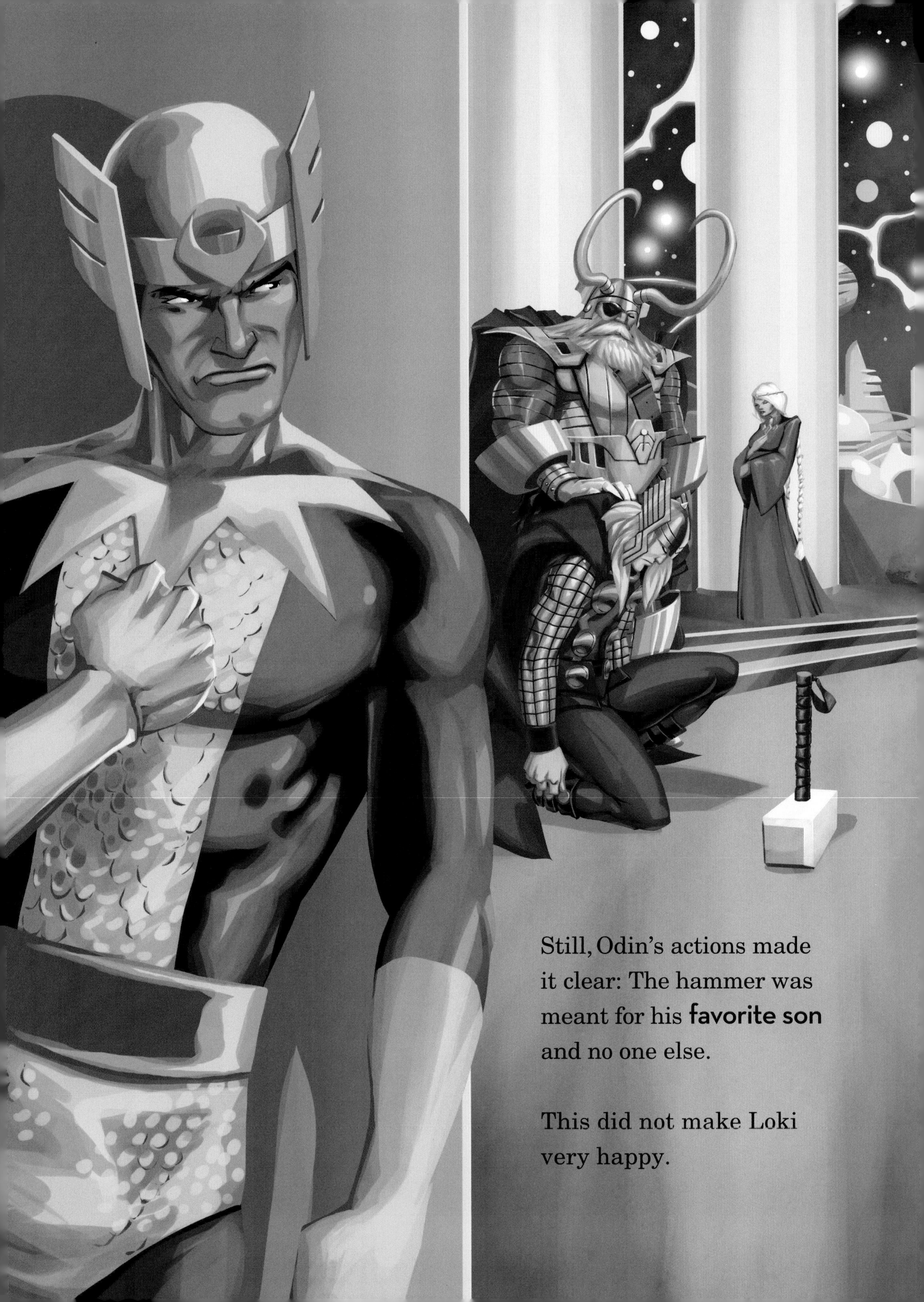

Still, Odin's actions made it clear: The hammer was meant for his **favorite son** and no one else.

This did not make Loki very happy.

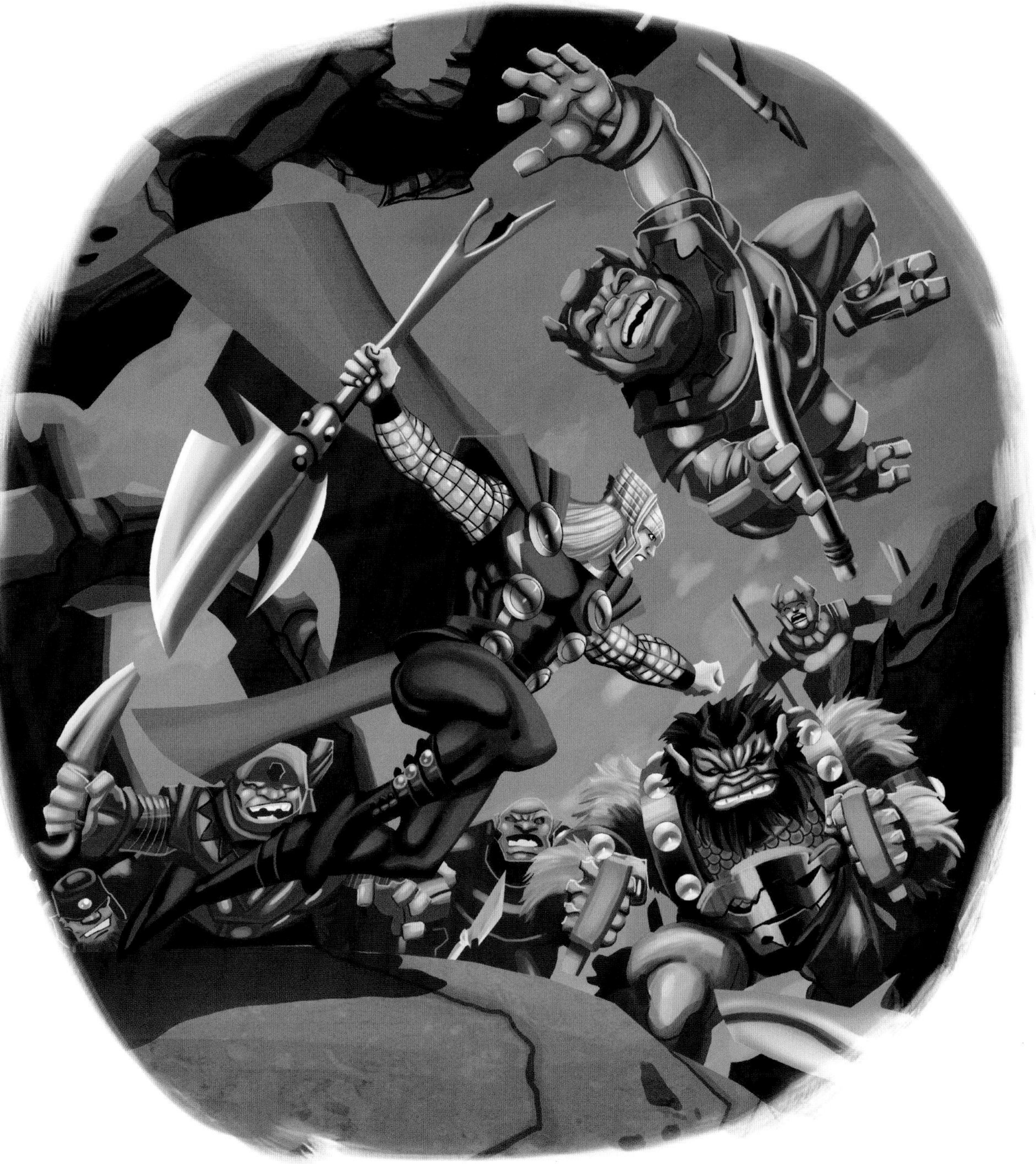

Even so, proving himself worthy of Mjolnir was not an easy task for Thor. He spent nearly every moment trying to earn his right to hold the hammer.

He performed amazing acts of **BRAVERY,**

NOBILITY,

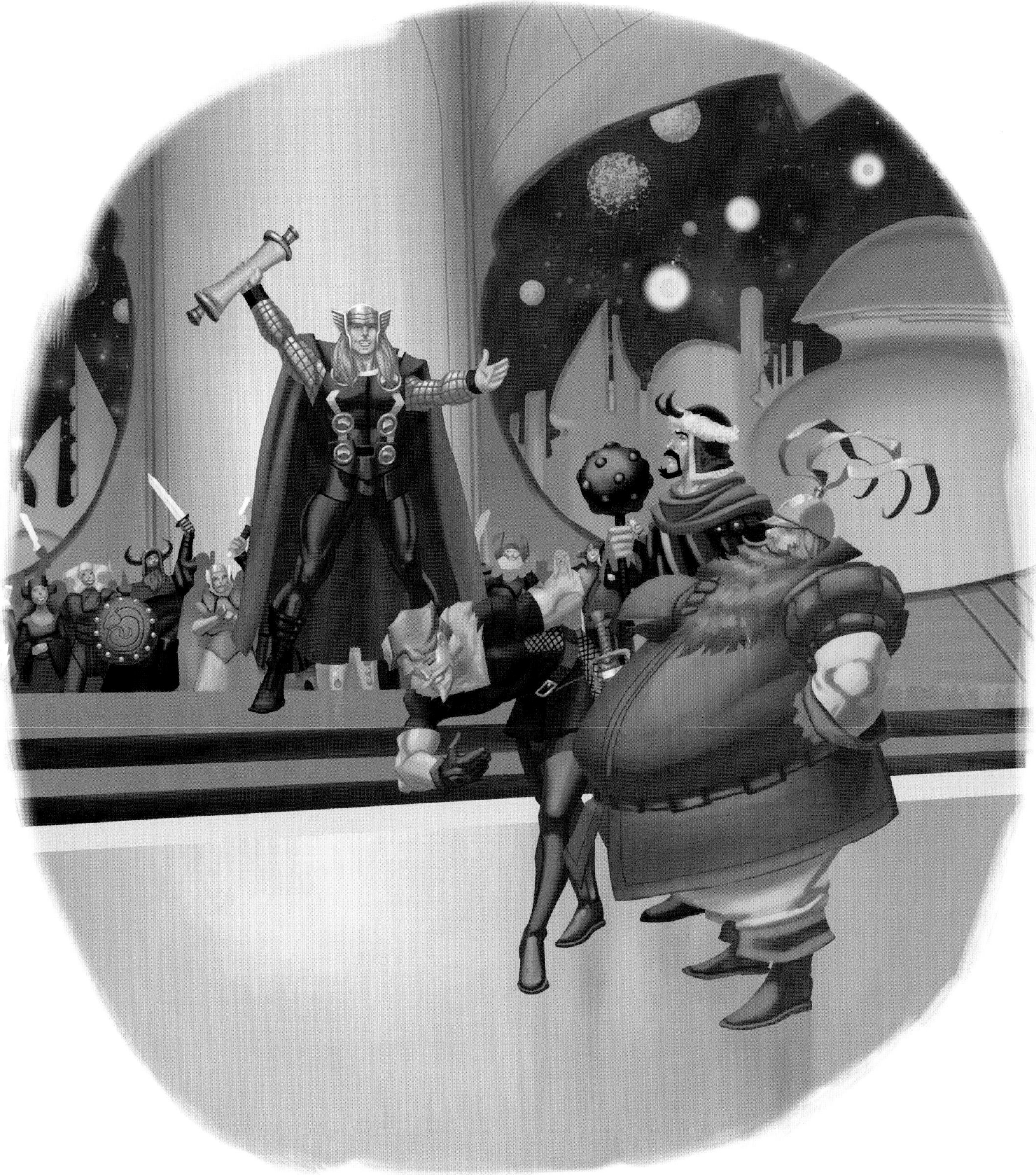

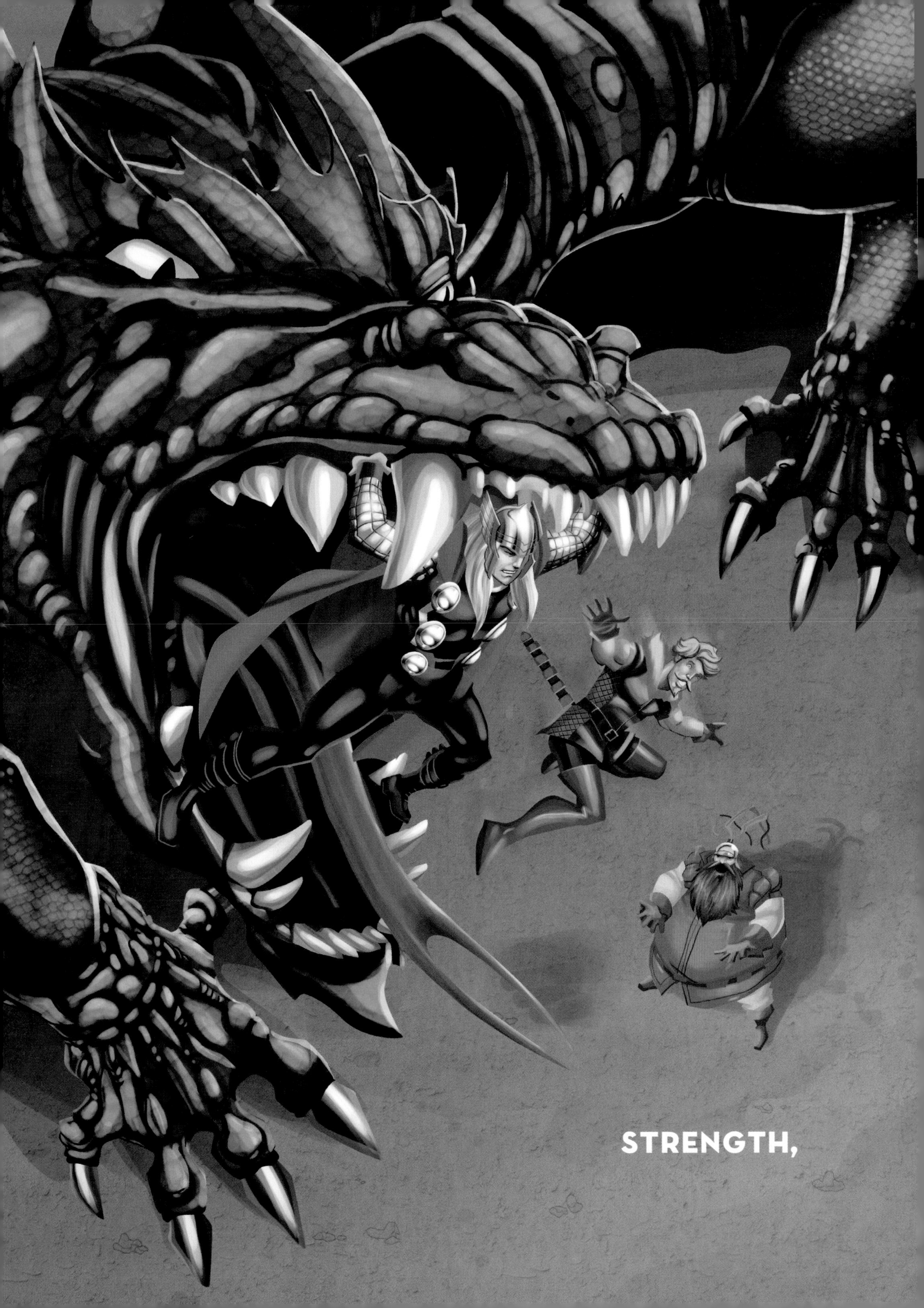

STRENGTH,

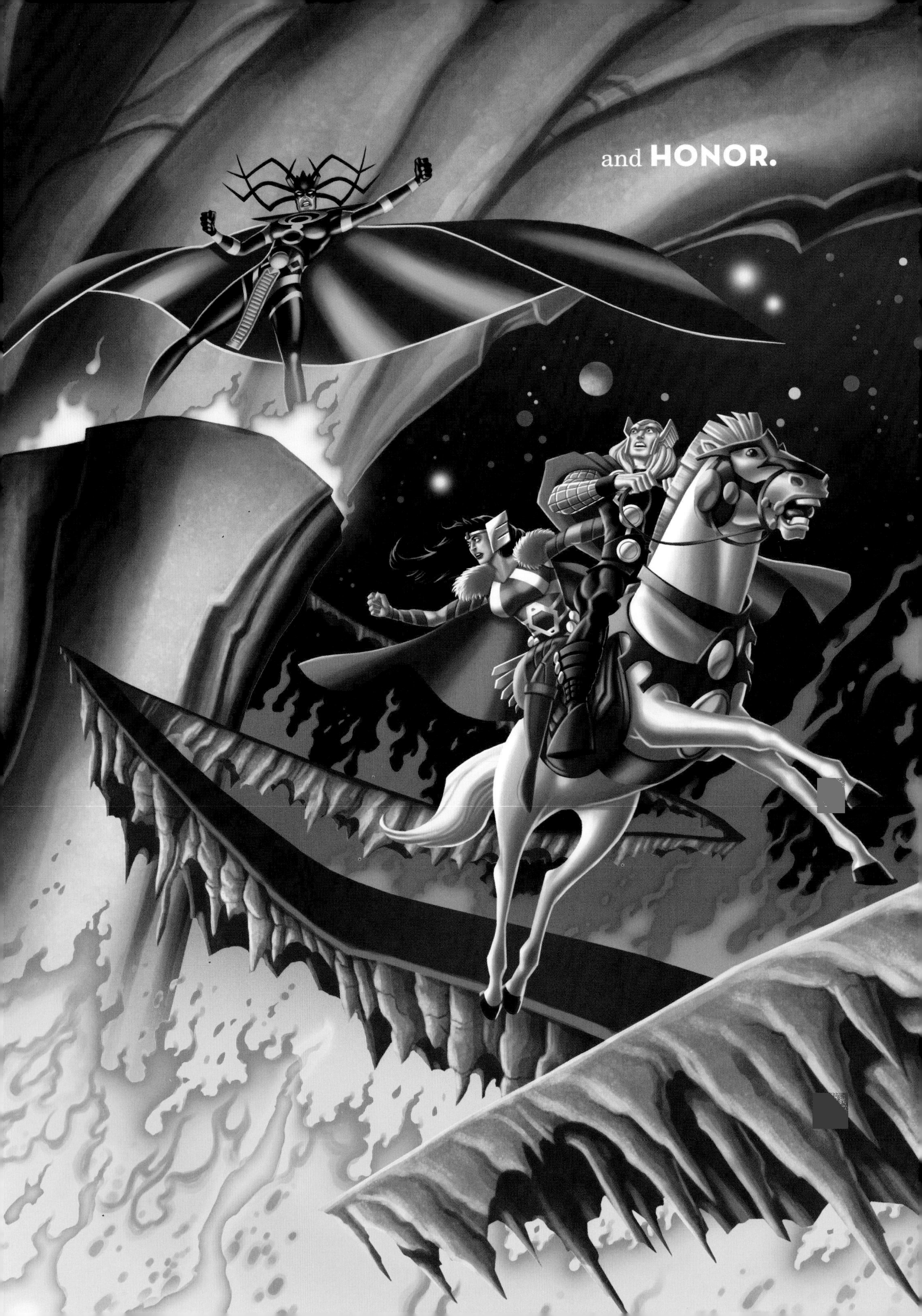

and **HONOR.**

With every great achievement, Thor attempted once more to pick up Mjolnir. It seemed as if he would never raise the hammer more than a few inches from the ground.

And then **one day . . .**

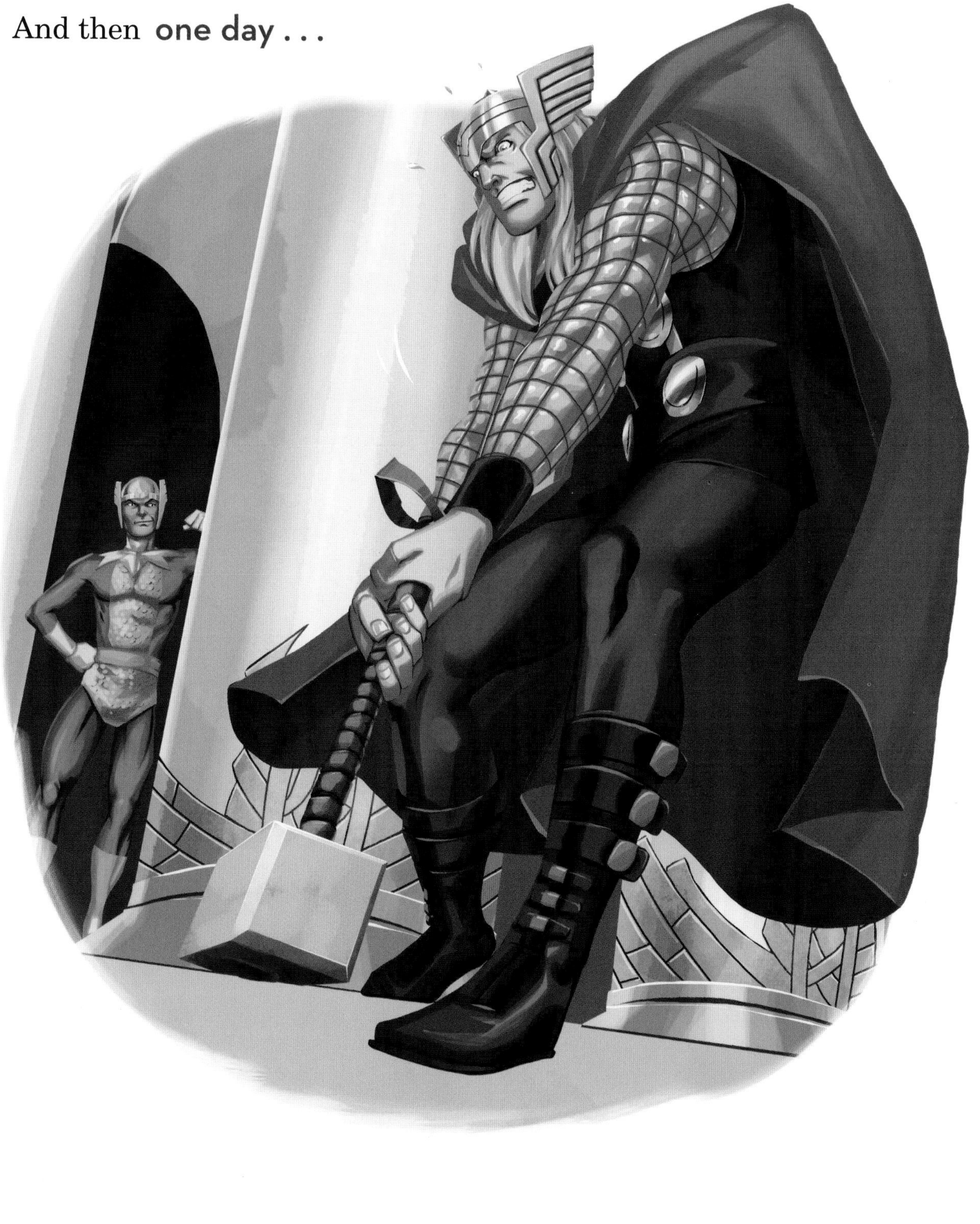

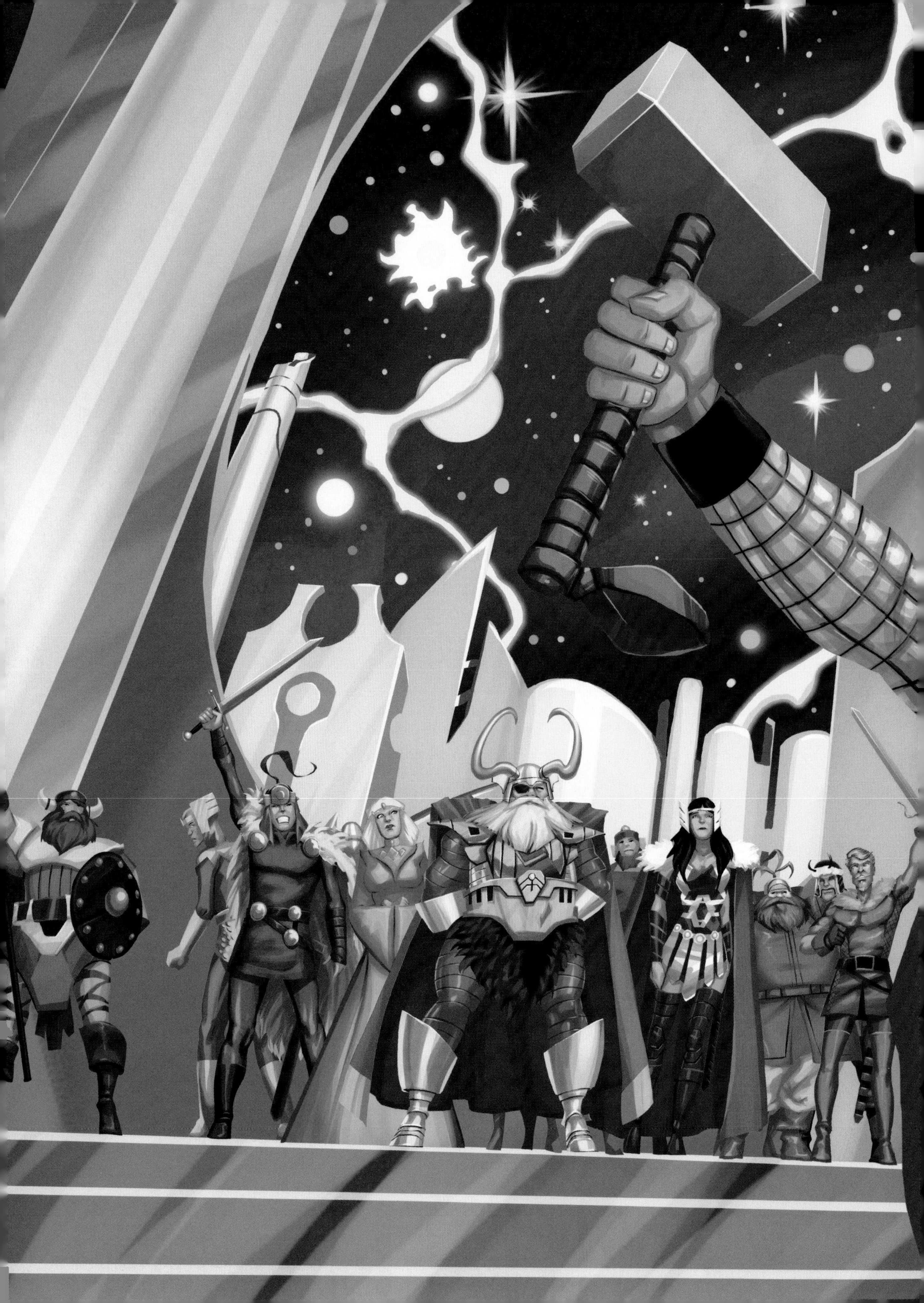

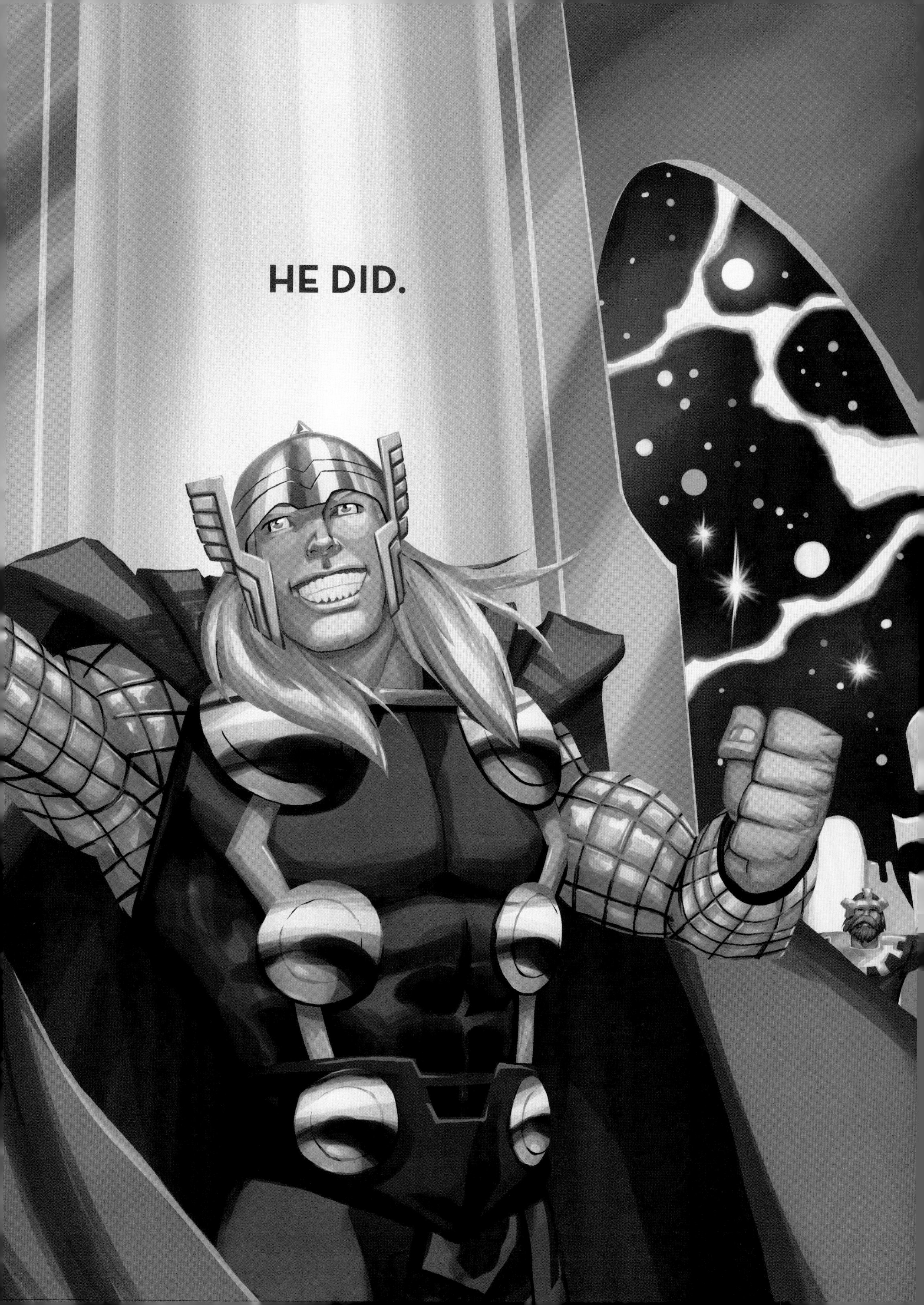
HE DID.

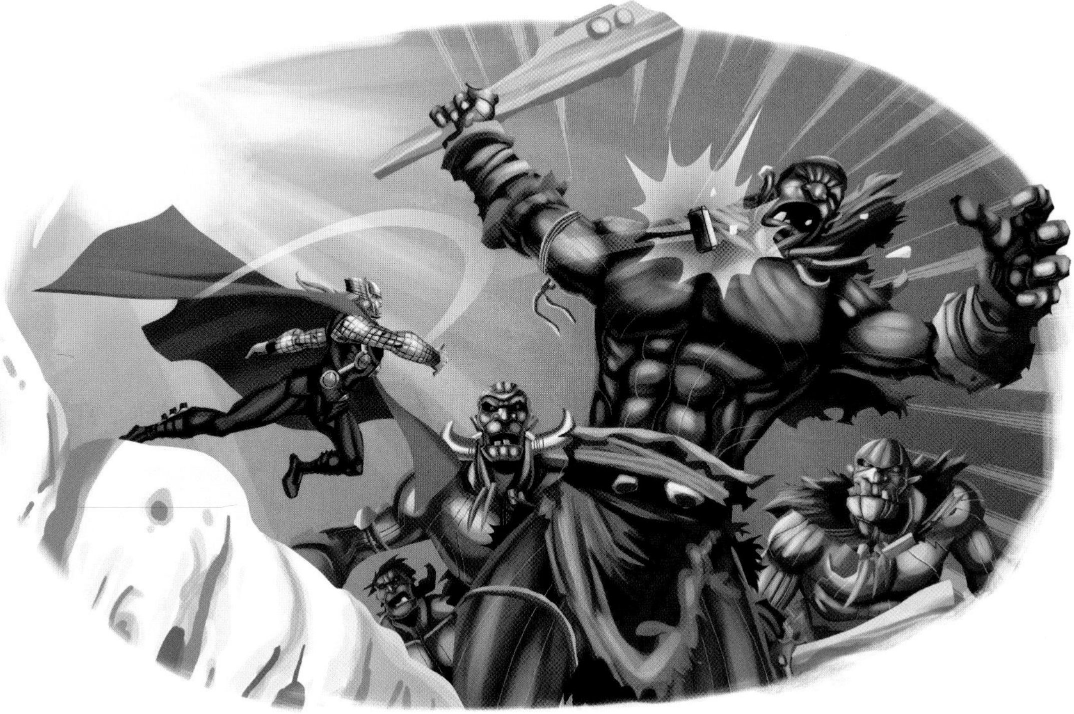

Thor had proven himself worthy of
his weapon, and he used it well.

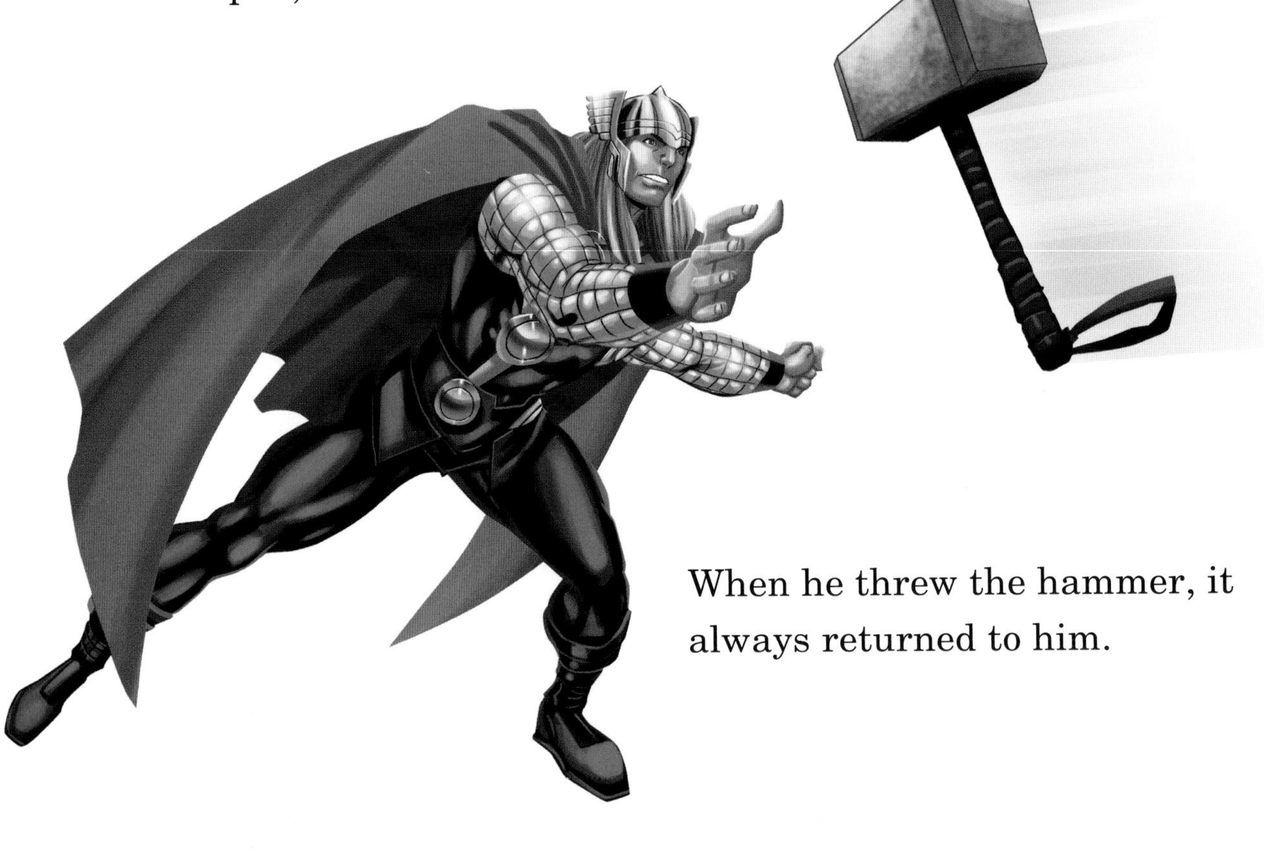

When he threw the hammer, it
always returned to him.

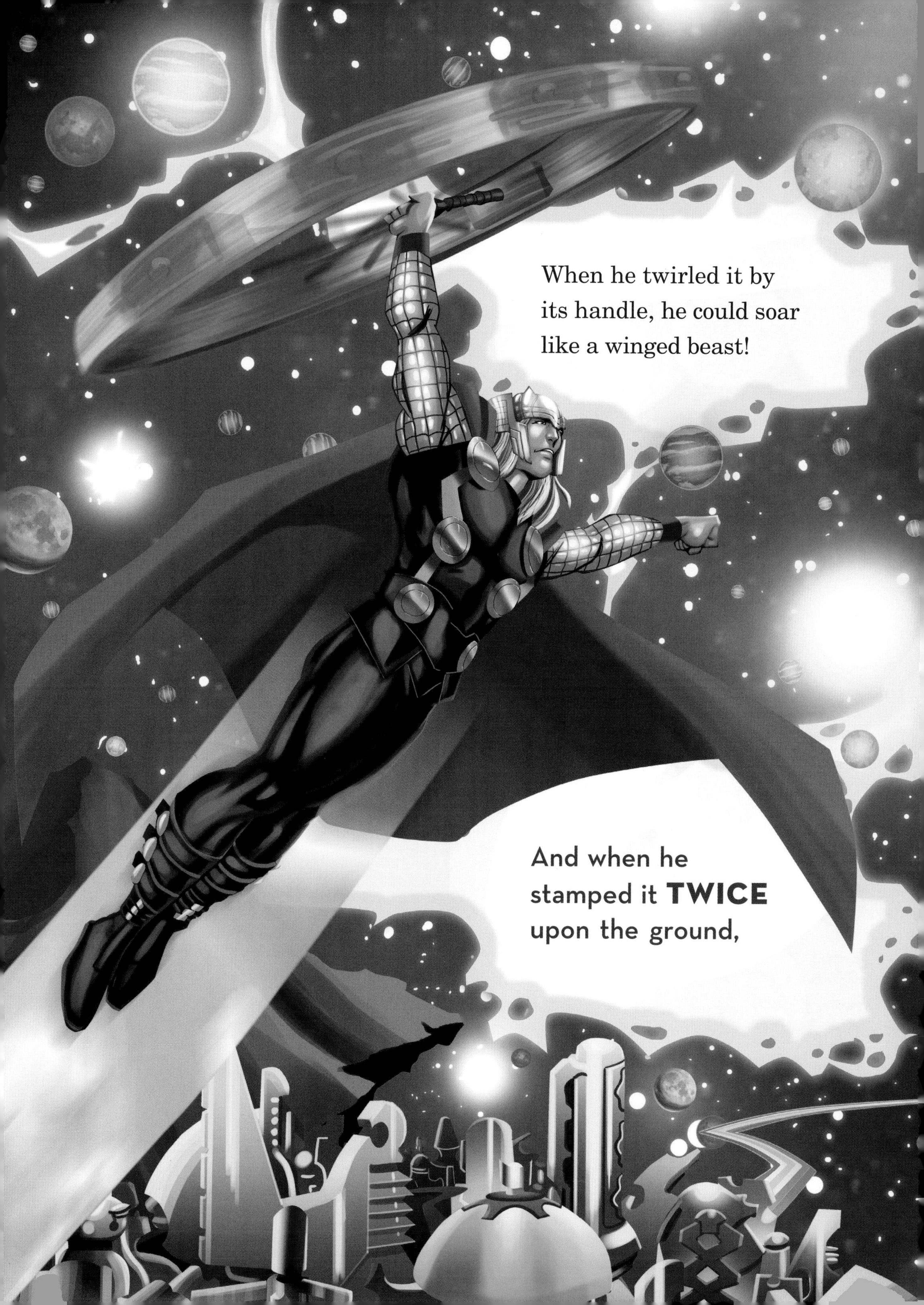

When he twirled it by its handle, he could soar like a winged beast!

And when he stamped it **TWICE** upon the ground,

he could summon all the power of **LIGHTNING, RAIN,** and **THUNDER!**

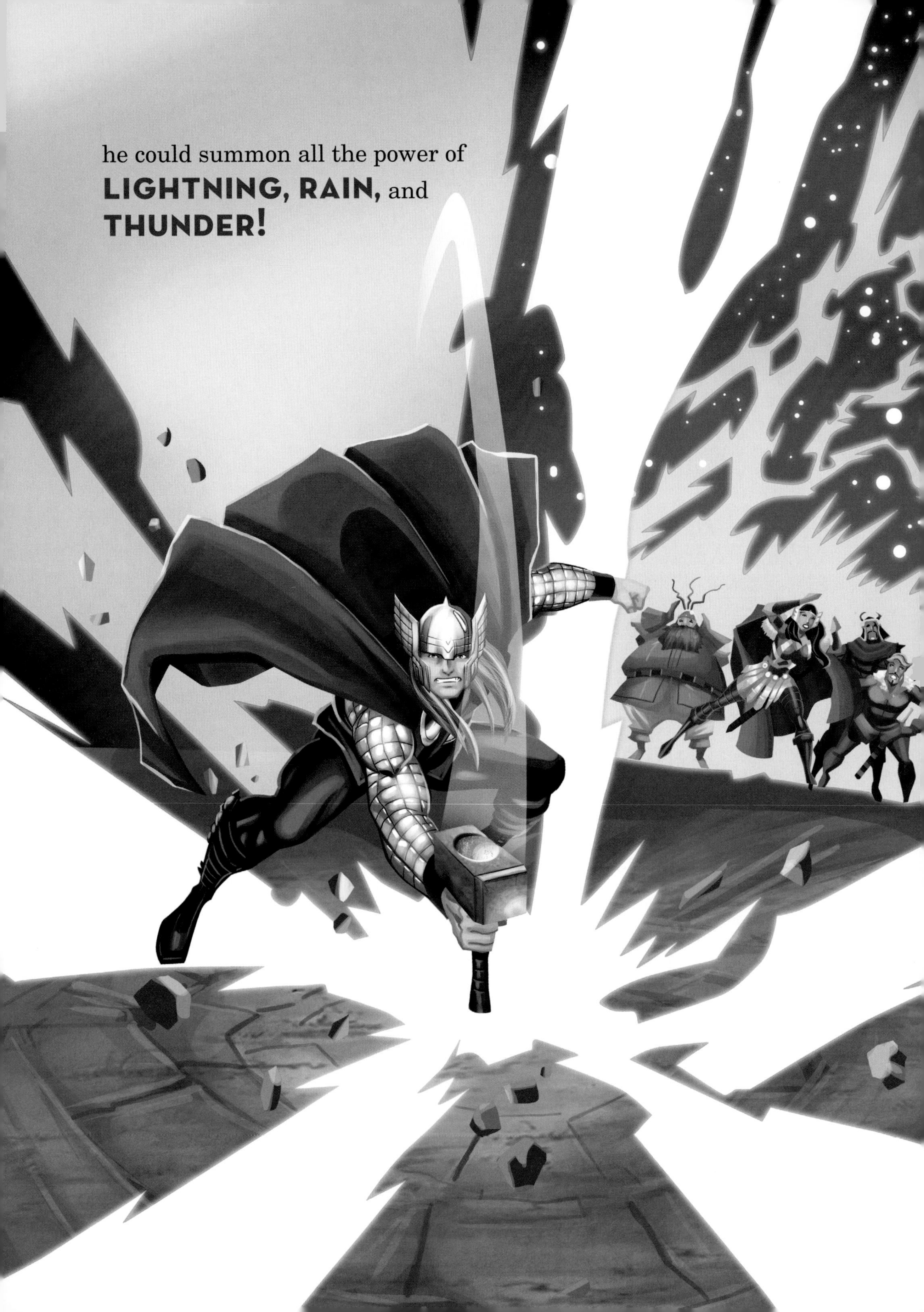

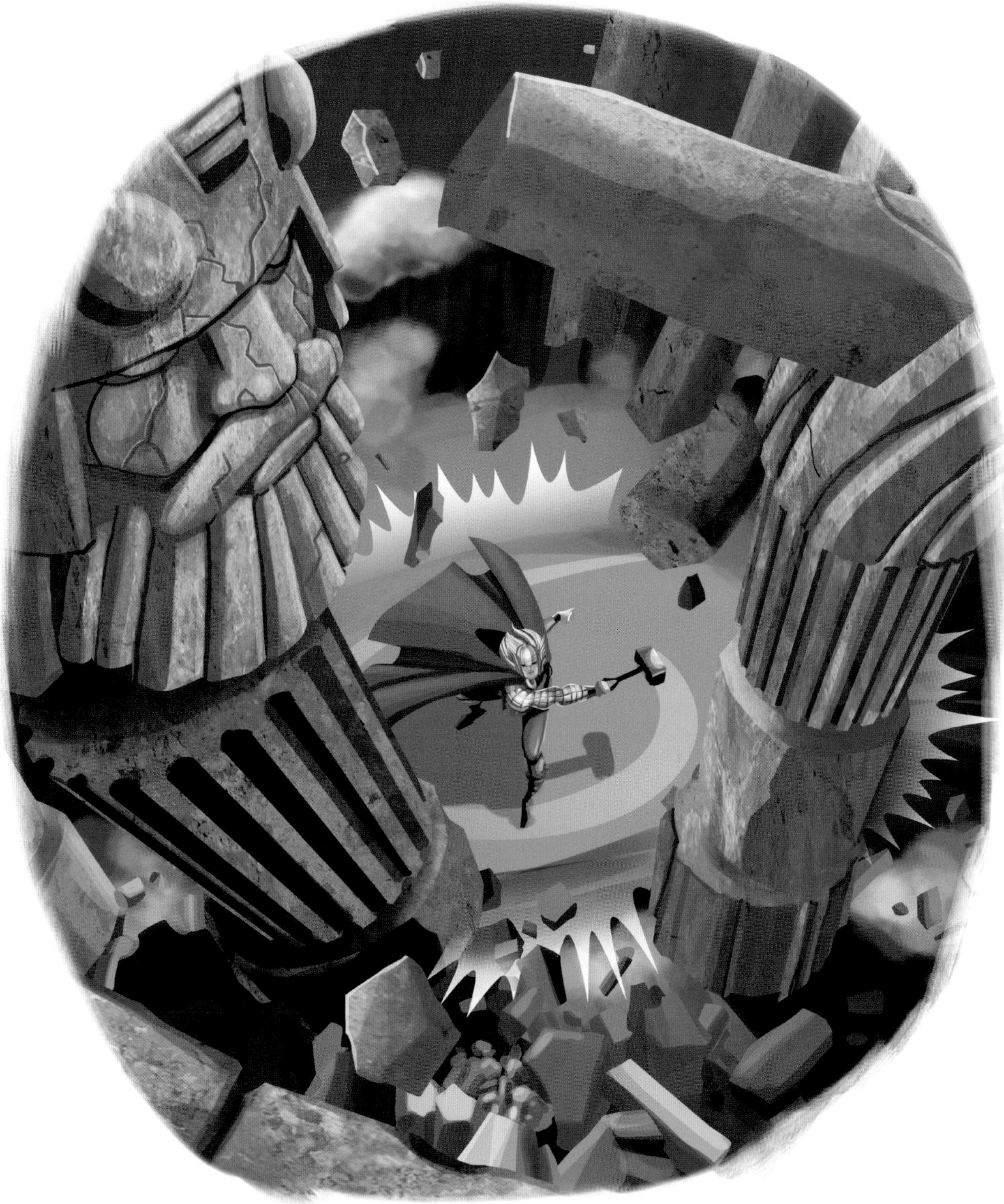

In fact, with his hammer in hand, there was
not much Thor could not do.

And he **knew** it.

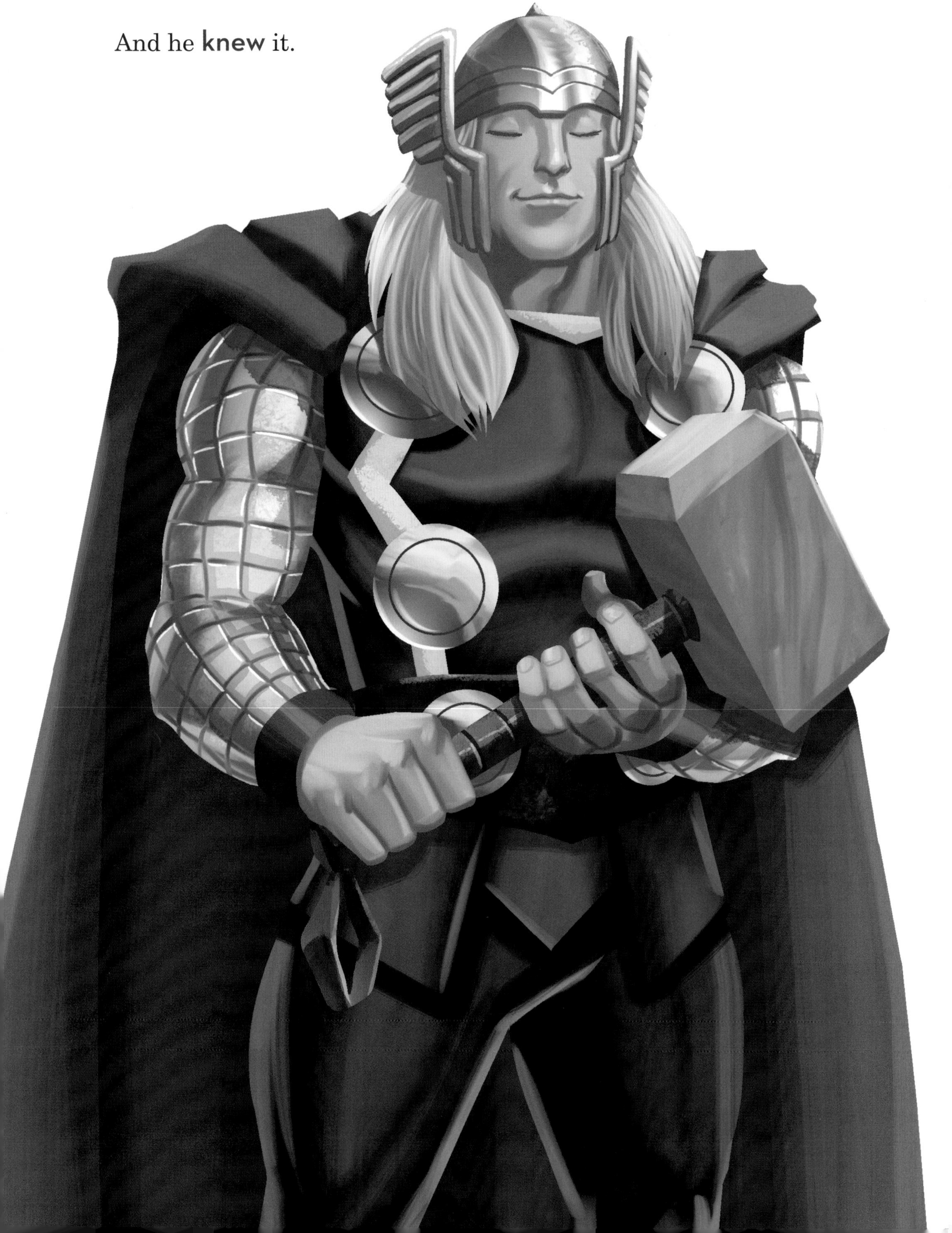

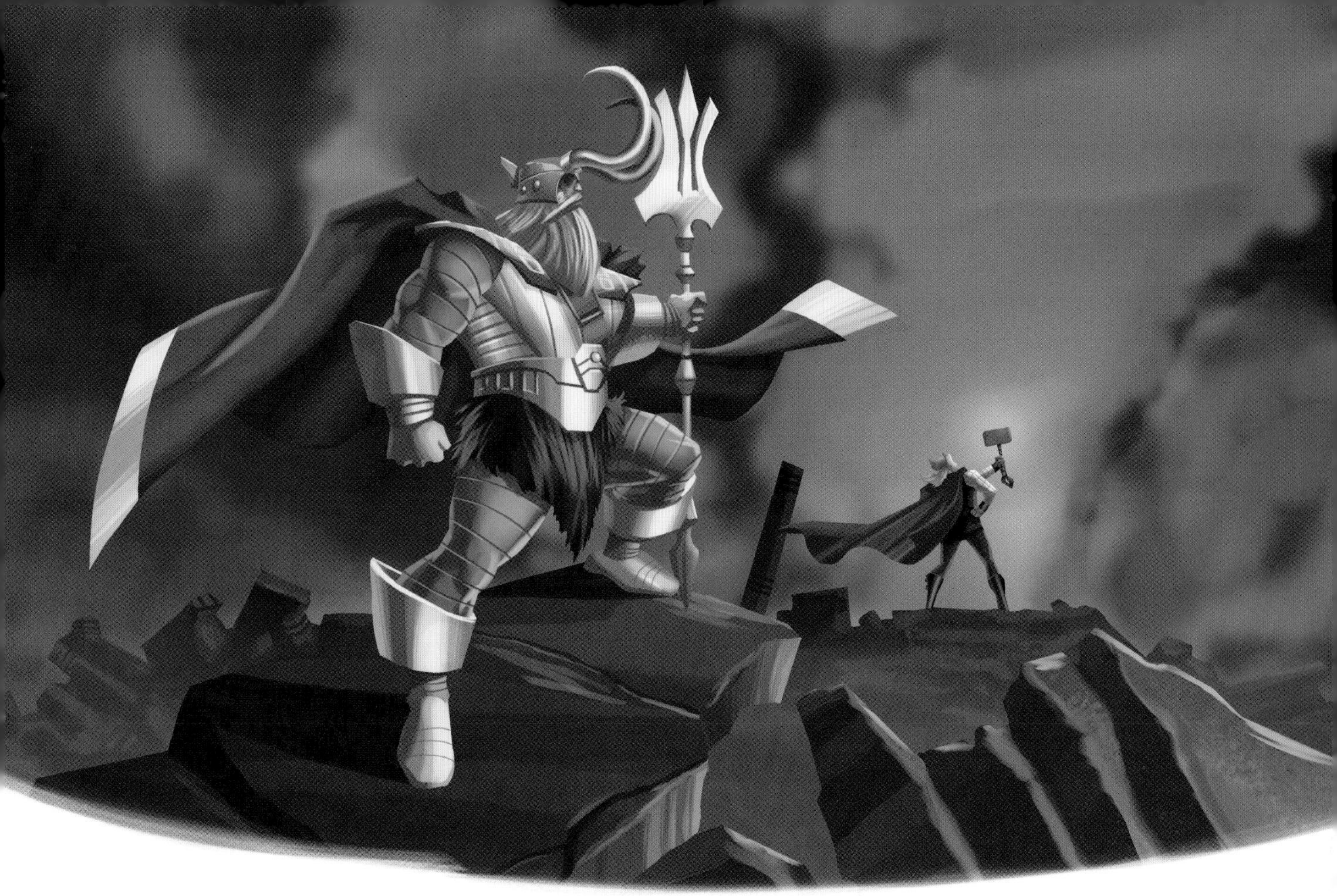

Thor thought he was doing everything right. Odin wanted him to be a great warrior, and he had become one. His father wanted him to earn the respect of Asgard. He had it.

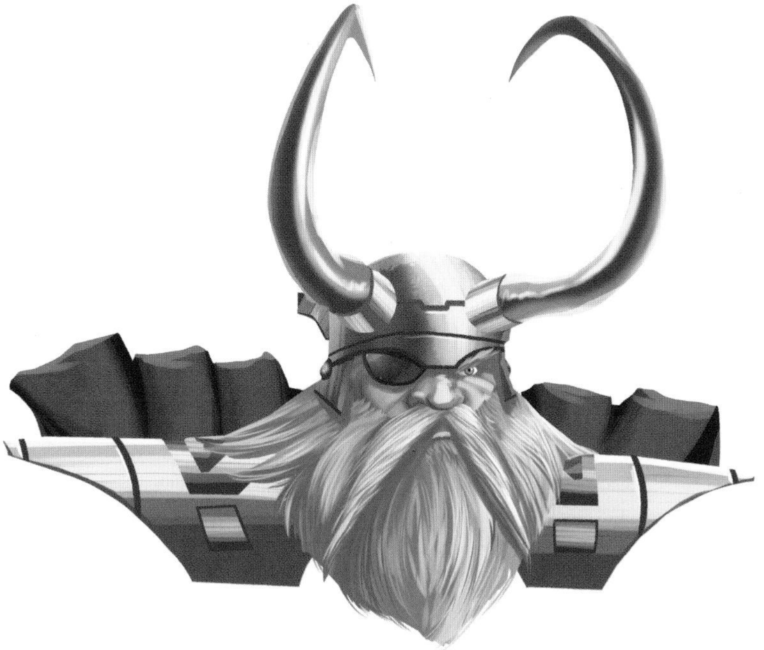

But then Thor began to let the power go to his head. And Odin was not happy.

In fact, he had grown quite angry with his son.

Odin called Thor to his throne room. Thor knew that **something was wrong.** His father rarely summoned him with such a harsh tone in his voice. Thor was sure that his **jealous brother** Loki had spun some **lie** to get him into trouble.

But there could have been nothing further from Thor's mind than what Odin had to say to him.

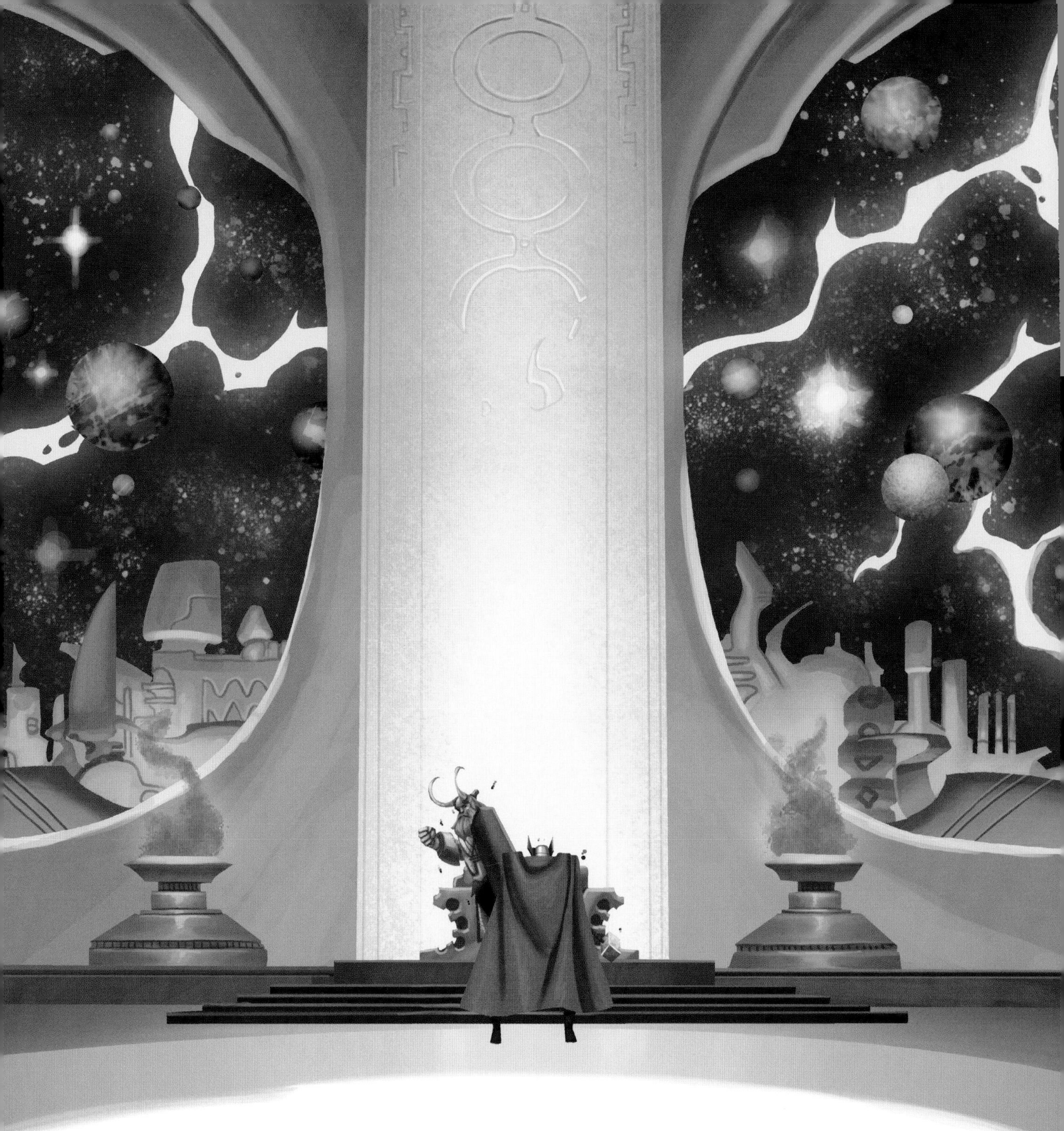

Odin told **Thor** that he was his **favored son.** He told him that he was brave beyond compare and noble as a prince must be.

He told him that his **strength** was **legendary** and that he was the **most honorable warrior** in the kingdom.

But Thor lacked *humility*. He did not know what it meant to be **weak,** or to feel **pain.** And without knowing those things, Thor could never be a truly **honorable** warrior.

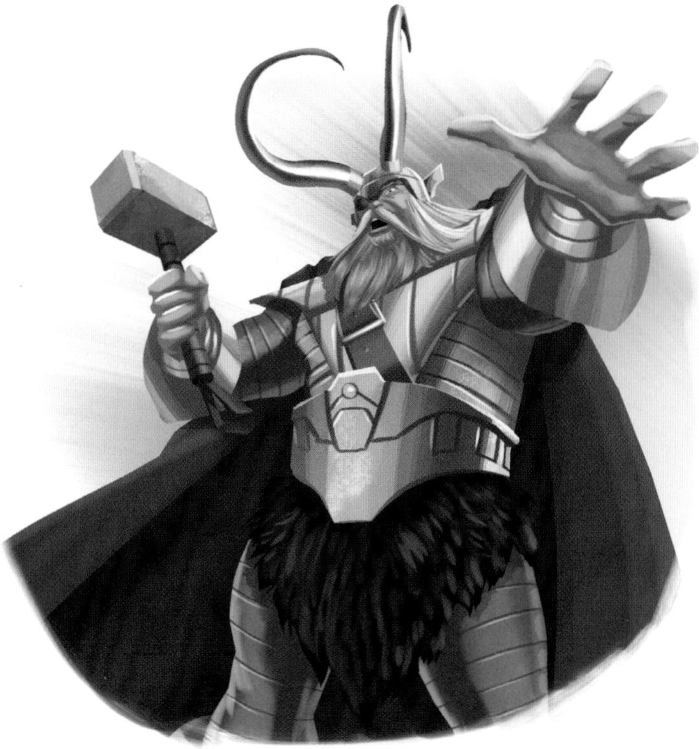

Odin, in his rage, tore Mjolnir from Thor's hand and threw it toward Midgard.

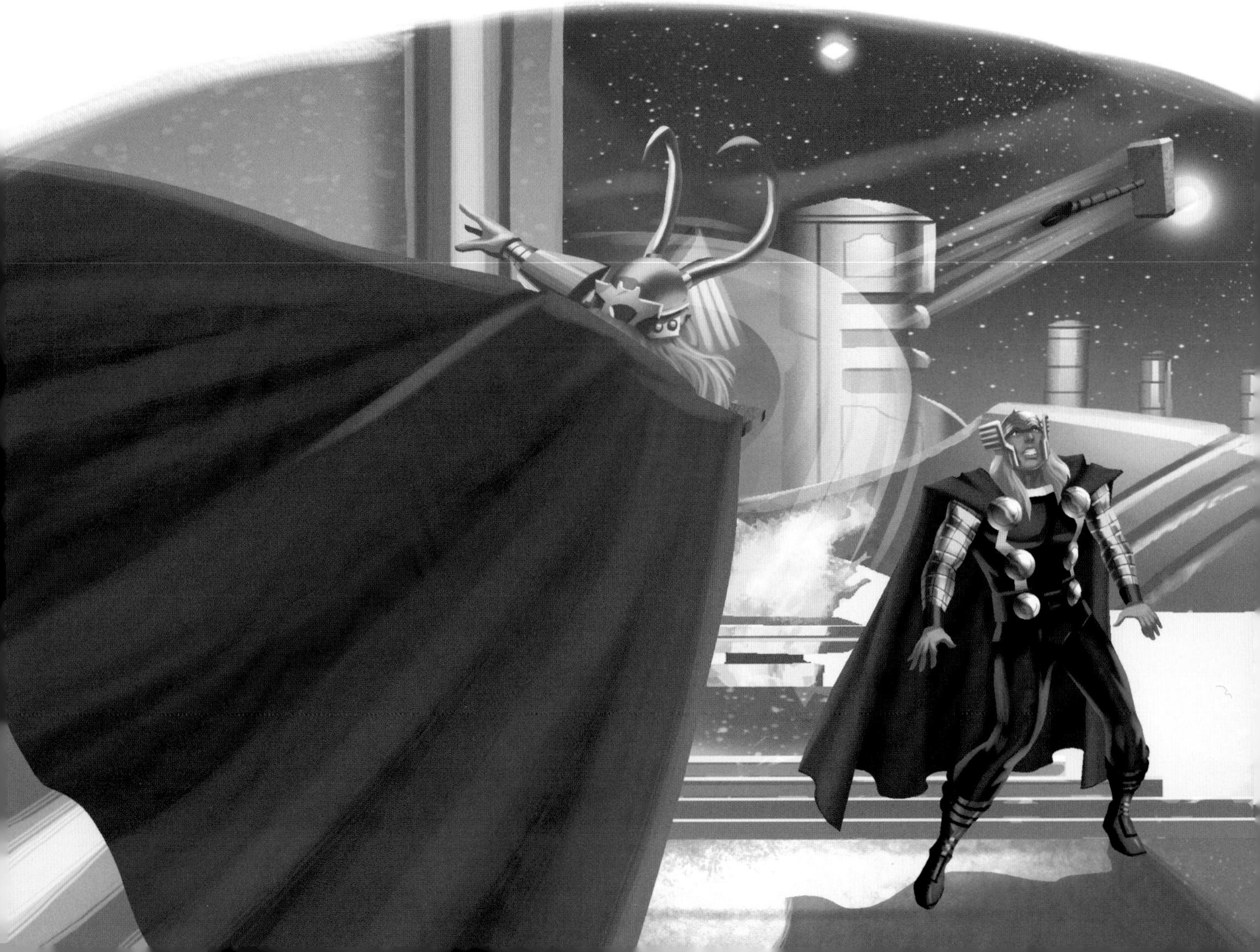

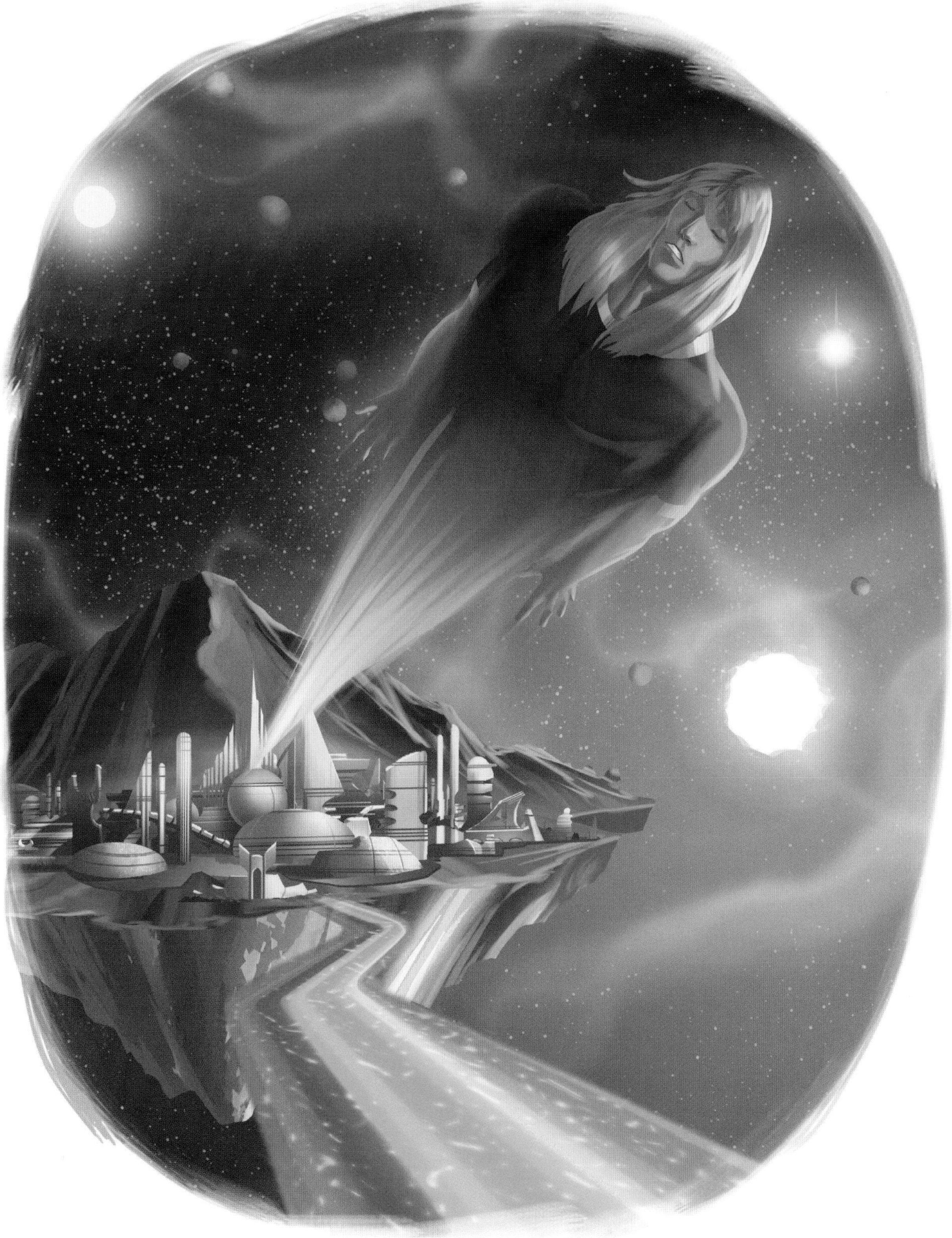

Then he stripped Thor of his armor and **sent him to Earth.**

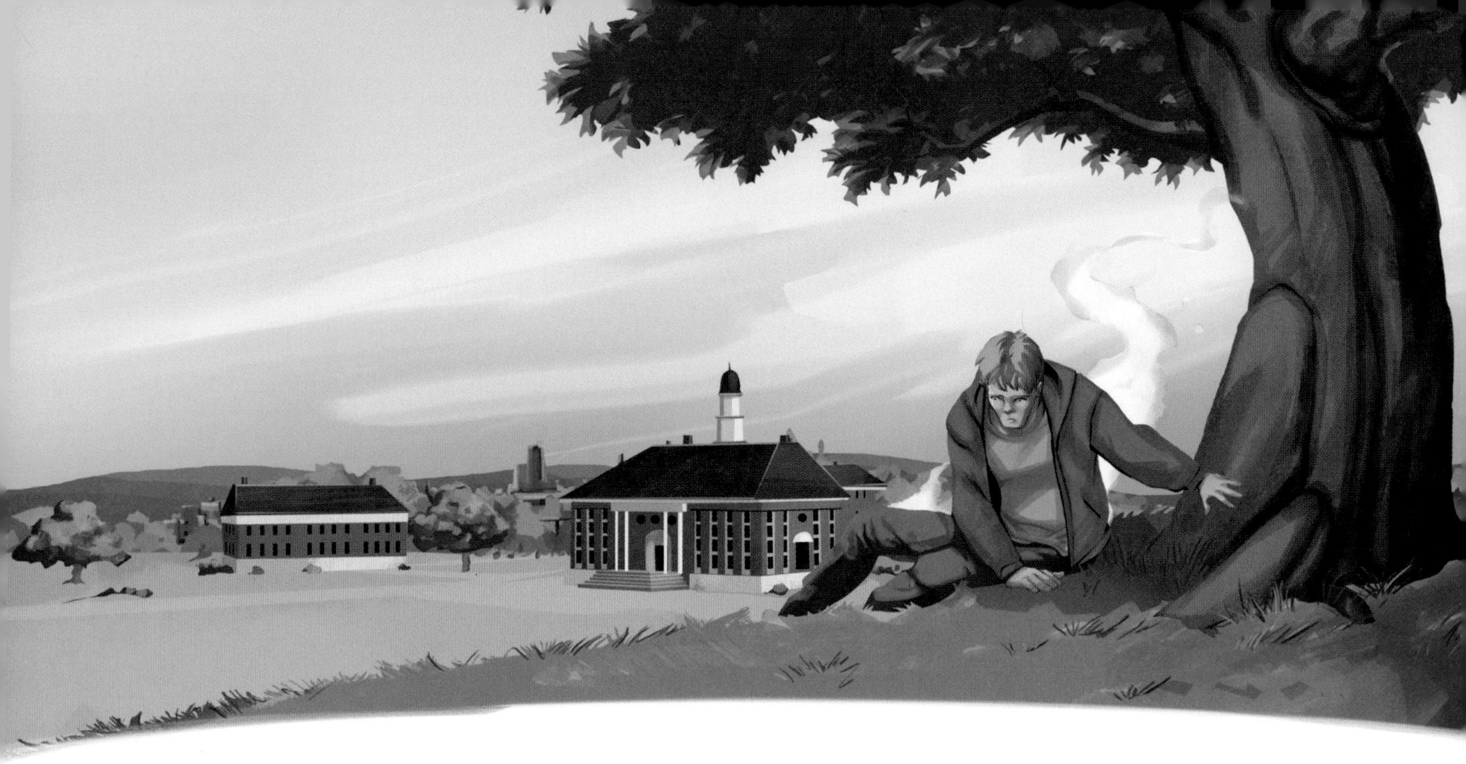

Thor's memory was wiped clean and he forgot his true identity. Instead, Odin made his son believe that he was a medical student with a crippling handicap named **DON BLAKE.**

As Blake, Thor learned to **study hard** in order to become a surgeon. At times he thought he might **fail.** But he worked harder than he ever had in Asgard, and in the end he **earned** his degree.

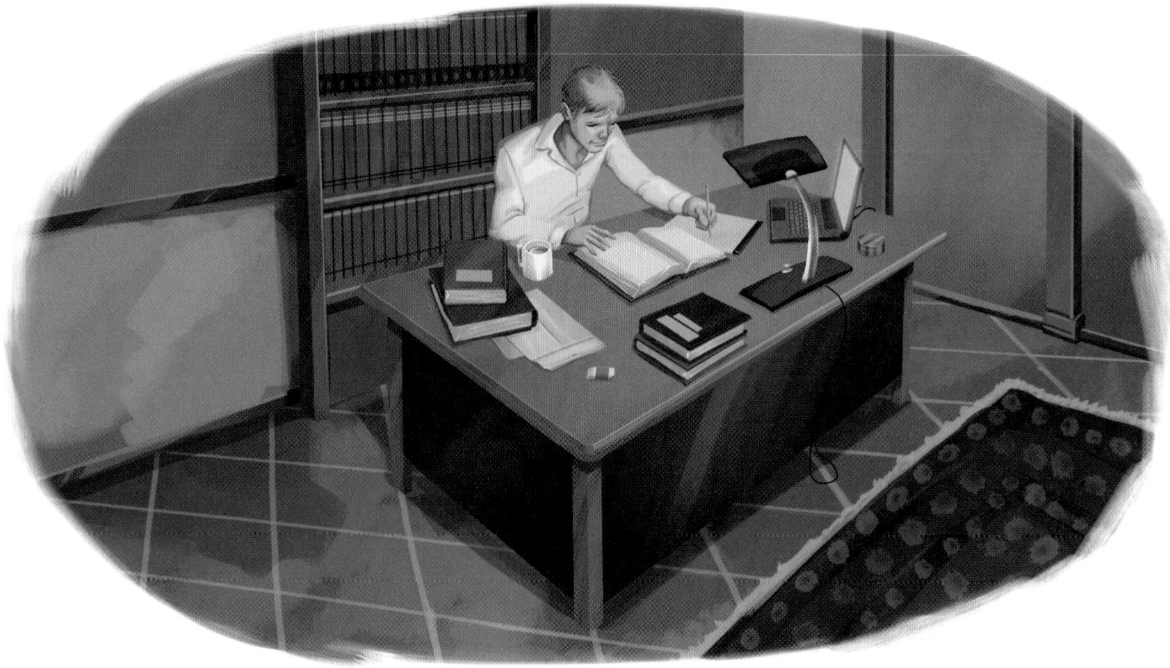

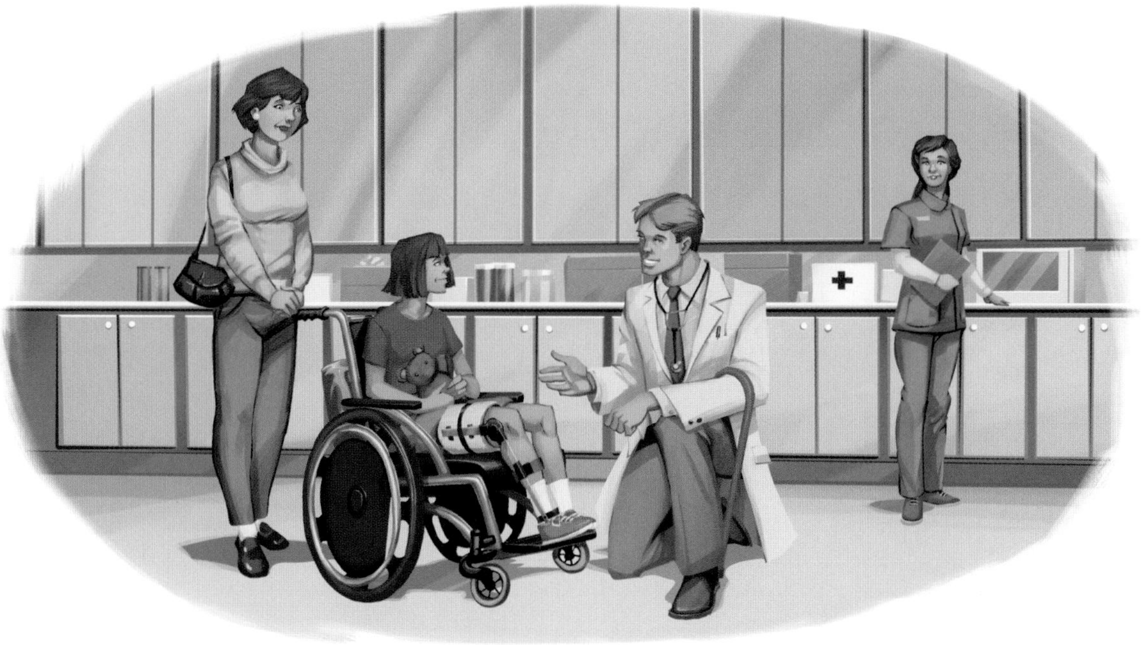

As a surgeon he treated the sick. He helped weak people find their **strengths.** He put others before himself and put his own life in peril if it meant he might **help** someone else.

And one day, while vacationing in Norway . . .

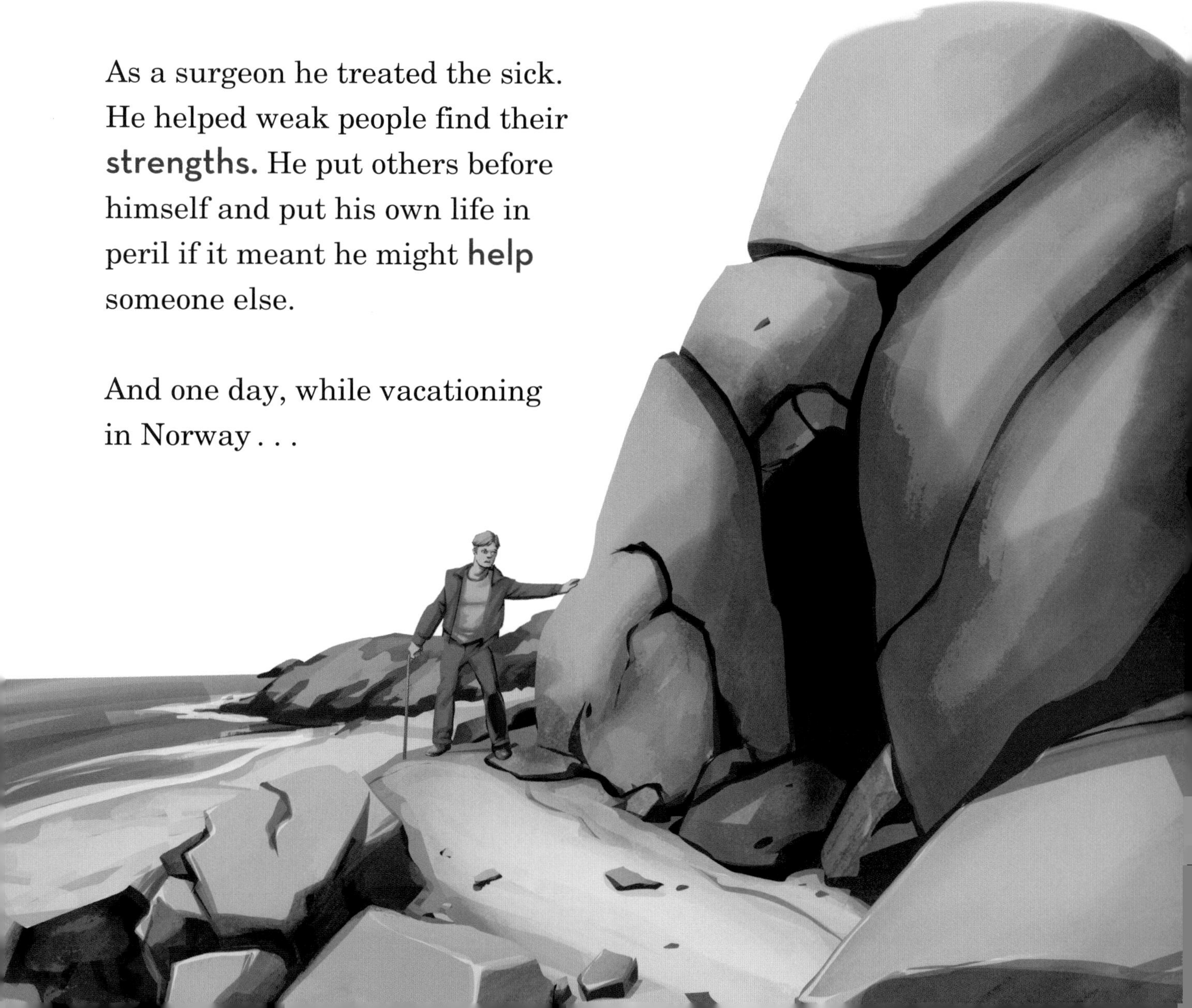

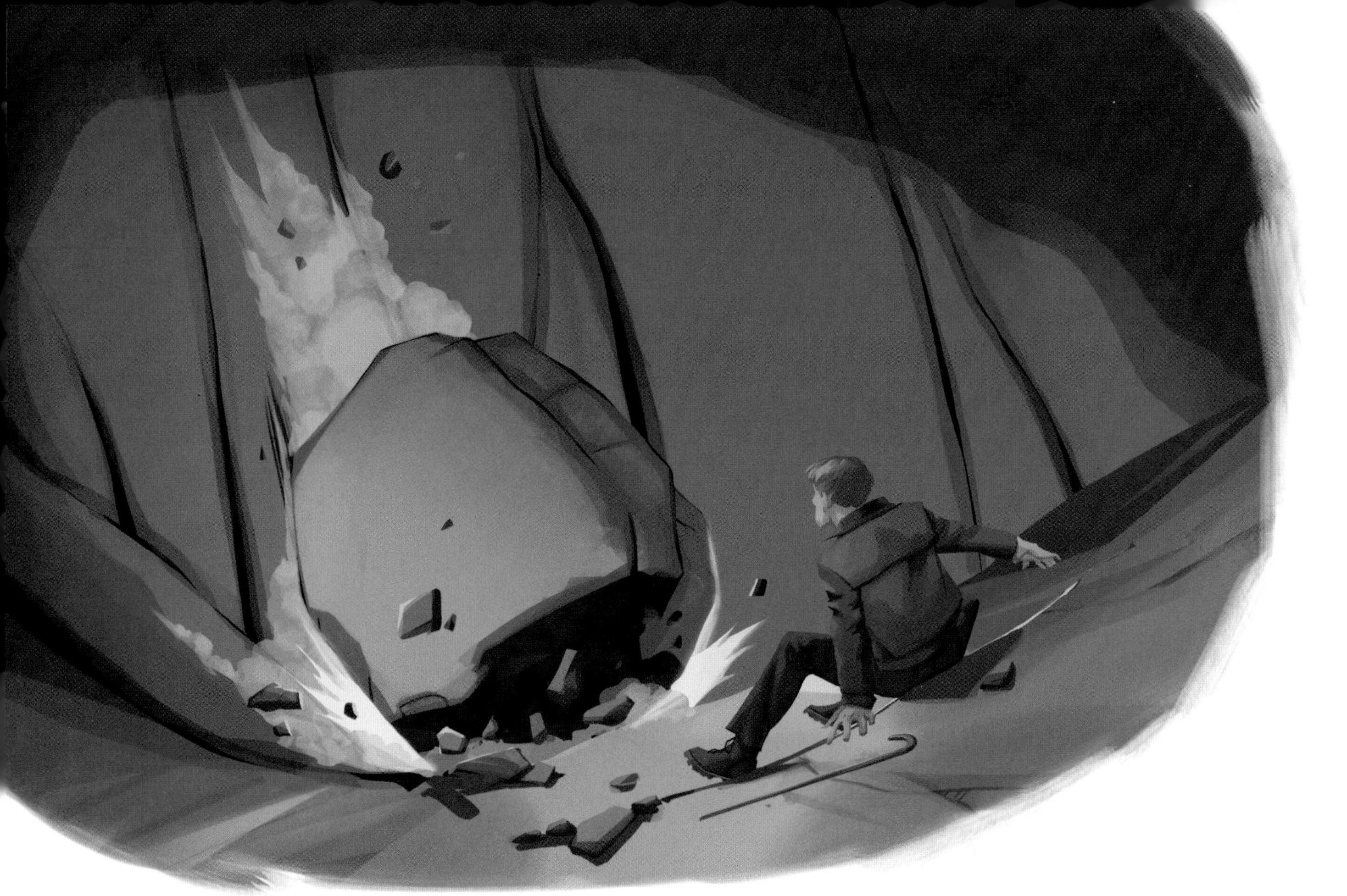

Don Blake found himself **trapped** in a cave.

The only possible exit lay behind a boulder.

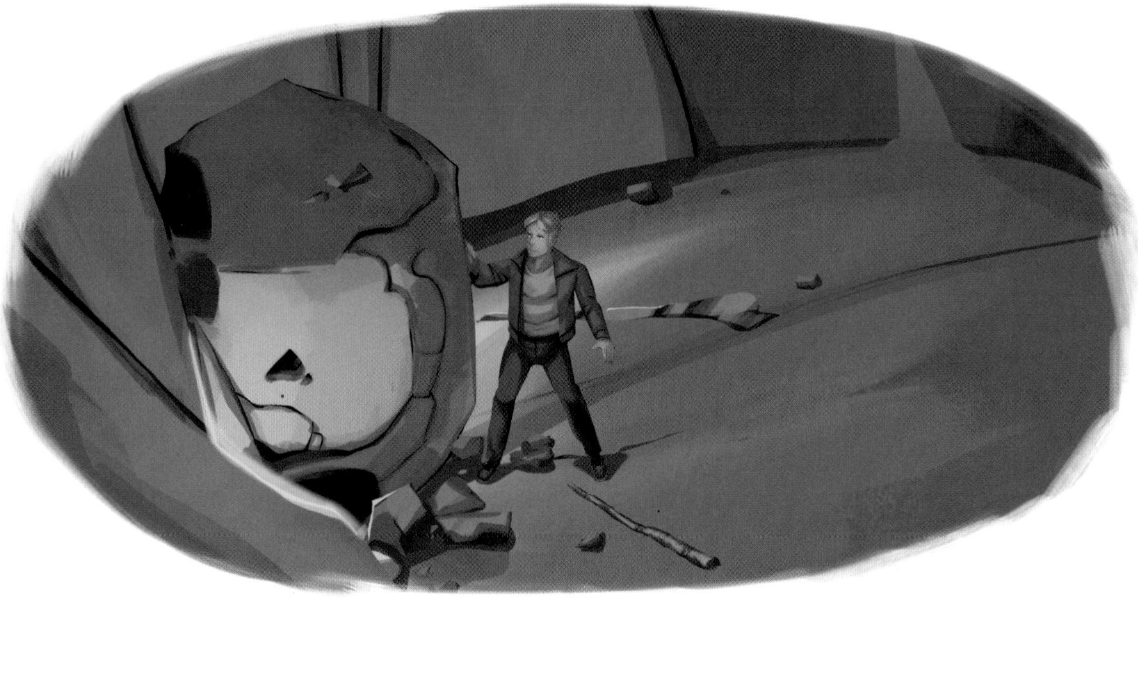

He found a staff on the ground and shoved it under the boulder. He tried with all his might to move the rock.

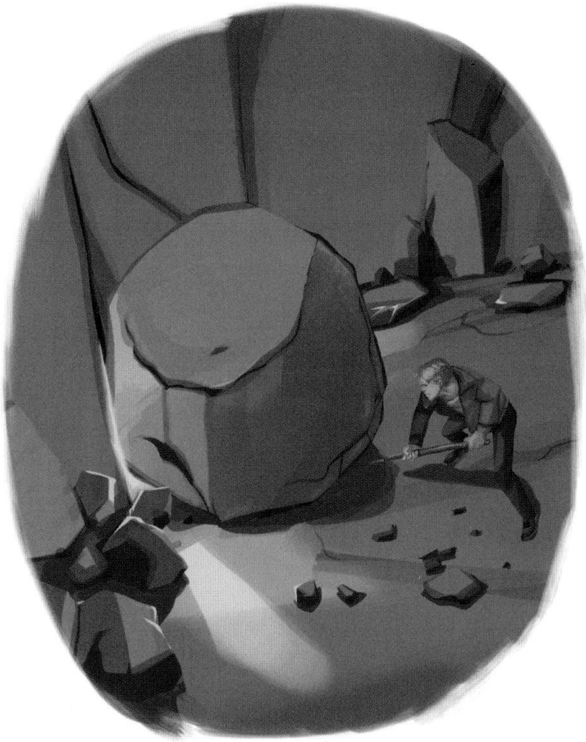

He pushed and pushed.

Nothing.

He was so angry that he took the staff and **struck** it on the ground. And that's when it became clear that it was no ordinary stick.

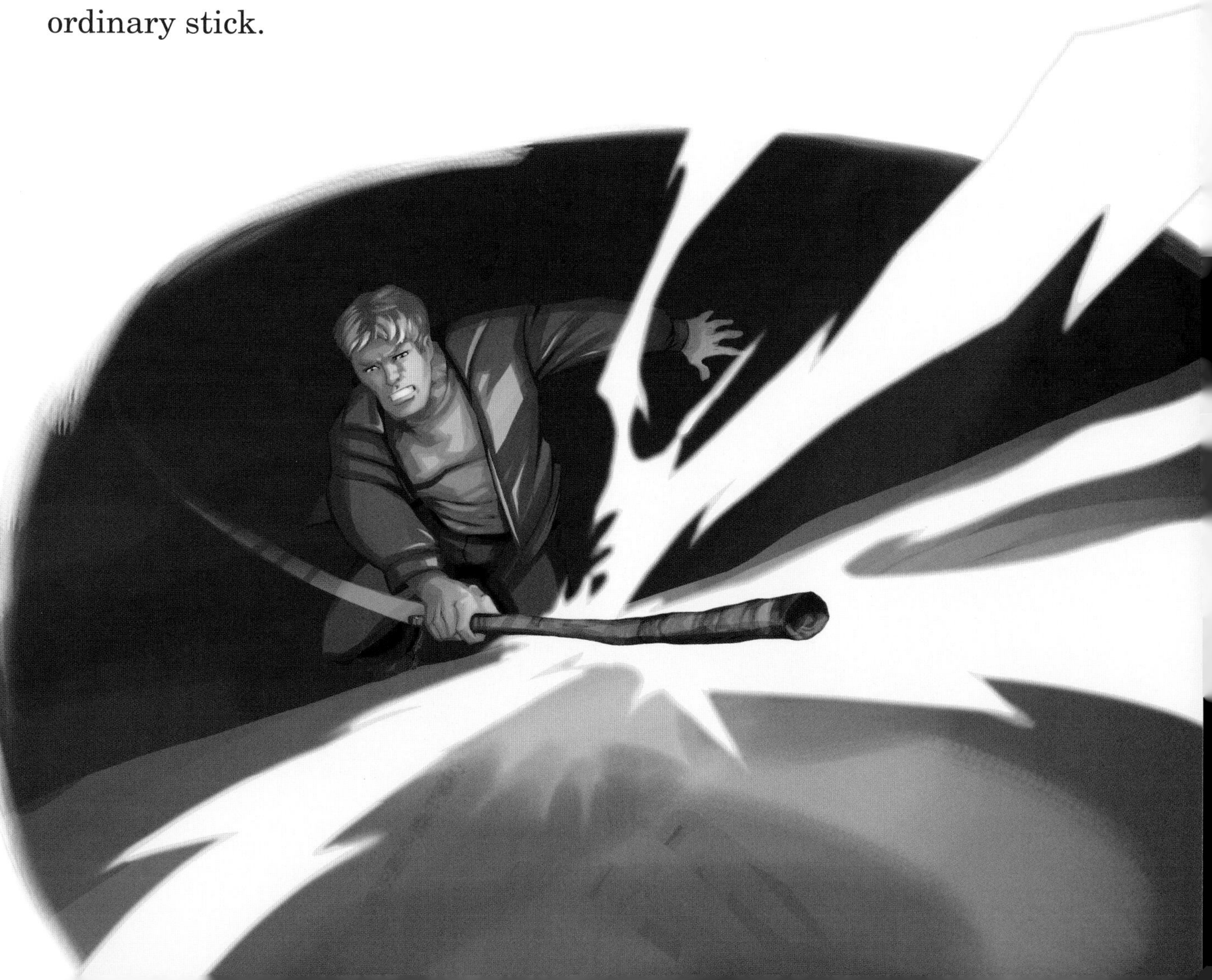

It was **MJOLNIR** in disguise!

Odin had sent Don to this cave.
Odin, the All-Father of Asgard,
was **pleased.**

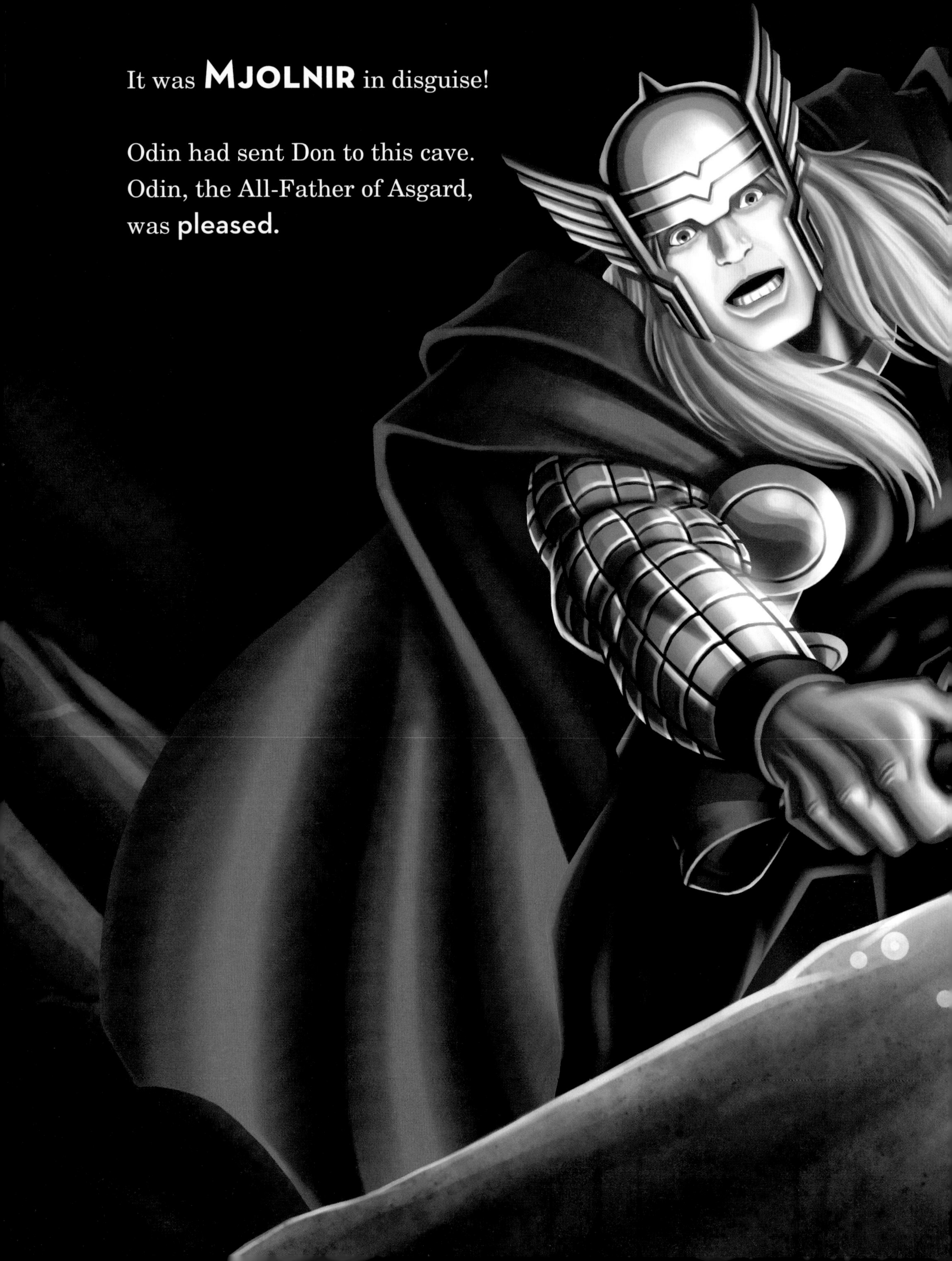

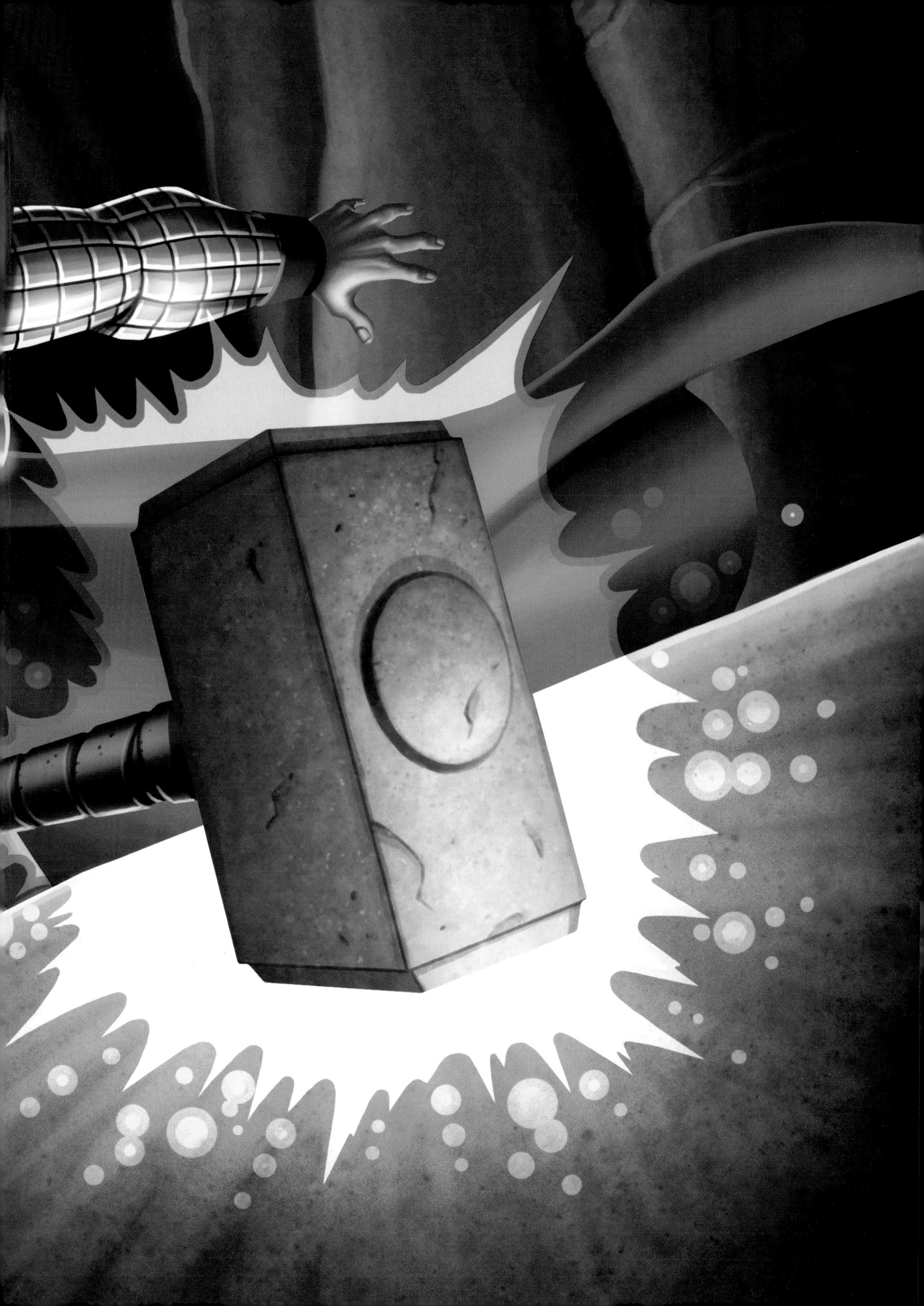

His son had learned **humility.** He had, at long last, become a complete **hero.** He had become **human** in spirit, but still, now and forever, he was

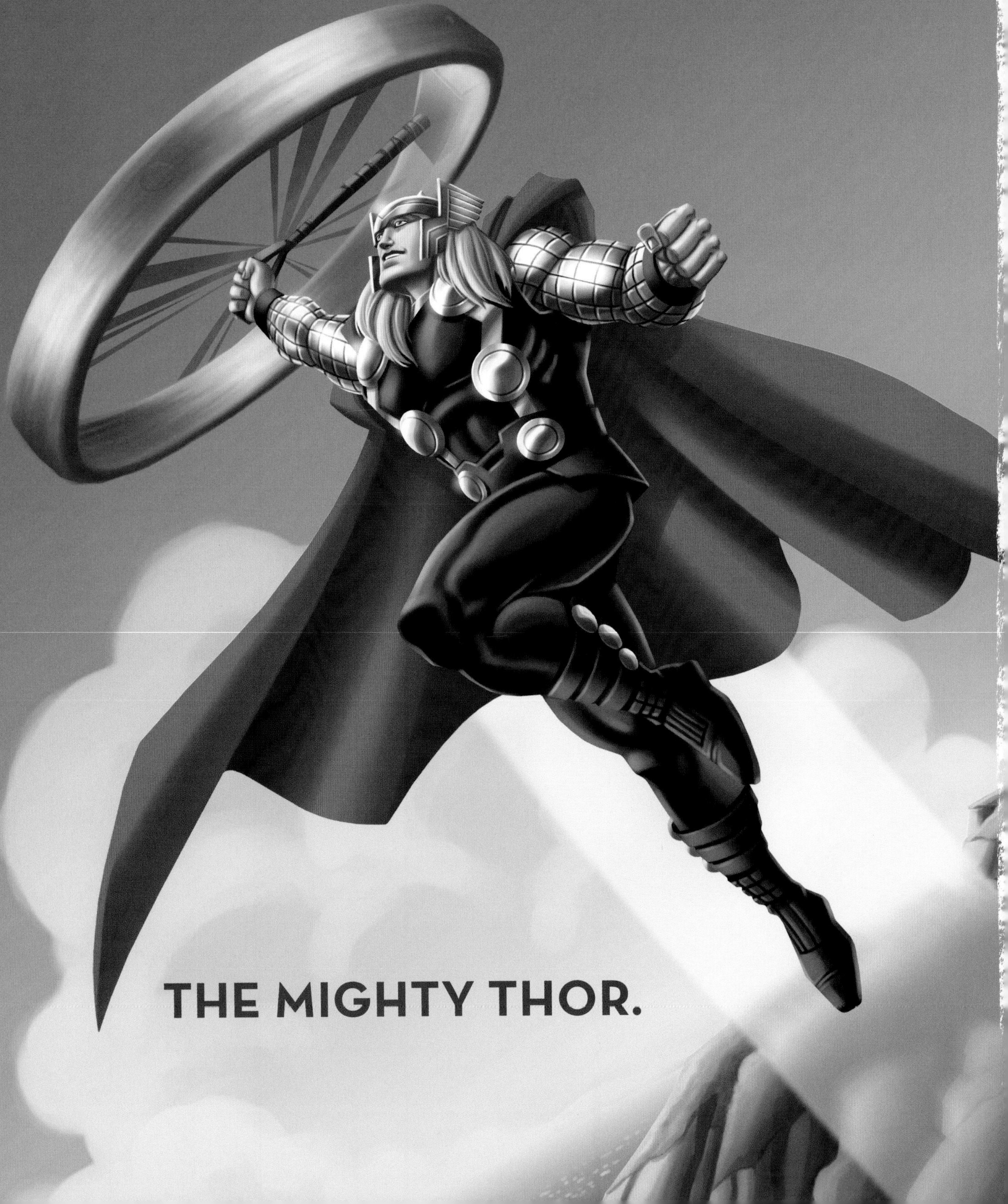

THE MIGHTY THOR.